To Dr. T.

The best ey

ever!

With gratitude,

Janet

July 2021

Rhubarb Pie

JANET THORNBURG

Thunderegg press

Thunderegg Press, LLC
P.O. Box 3023
Eugene, OR 97403
www.thundereggpress.com

Some of these stories originally appeared
in the following publications:
"Pink Rods, Red Clouds, and a Rhubarb Pie" in *Carve Magazine*
and *The Best of Carve Magazine*, Volume Four;
"First Date" in *Lumina;* "Lucky Lady" in *The MacGuffin;*
"Meat" in *The Distillery* and *The Noe Valley Voice;*
"Chosen" in *Phantasmagoria;* "In My Neighbors' Garden"
in *In The Family;* "Zephyr" in *Phoebe*.

Library of Congress Control Number: 2005904799

ISBN 0-9725096-1-5

Book and cover design by Helen Liu
Cover photo by Janet Thornburg
Text set in Goudy

Printed in the United States of America
10 9 8 7 6 5 4 3 2 1

These stories are for

Michelle, Nick, and Sarah

and for my mother

Contents

Pink Rods, Red Clouds, and a Rhubarb Pie

Effie Cunningham — Friday

Imogene was out of breath when she came into the shop, and that should have been my first clue. She is not a small woman, and she is not one to go trotting about. I didn't pay it much mind, though. I was busy getting out the curlers for her perm. I needed a lot, because Imogene likes a tight curl. She has kept the same hairstyle ever since she moved to Red Cloud from Guide Rock sixteen years ago, right after she married Marv Banks. She says that's how her hair was when Marv fell in love with her, so why mess with a good thing?

As soon as I got her leaned back into the shampoo sink, she said, "Raise me back up Effie, and bring me a glass of water, would you?" Well, I cranked her back up, but I was wondering why she hadn't asked me ahead of time. When I came out of the back with her water, she was craning her neck toward the window, looking up Main Street.

"What's the matter, Imogene? Somebody after you?" I asked her. She didn't laugh. That was not like her either because

Imogene always likes a good joke. This afternoon, though, she just said, "Let's get started on that perm. I got to be out of here by 5:00."

Well, it was no skin off of my nose. That'd give me an extra half hour to put my feet up before my next appointment, but it did seem odd. A perm and do always takes at least two and a half hours with Imogene because of all those tiny red and blue rods I use on her.

"I'll do it, Imogene, but I'm going to have to use the pink rods. That's going to make your perm a little looser, and your hairdo isn't going to look quite the same. If you wake up tomorrow and don't like the look, we're out of luck because that Willa Cather conference is starting up, and you know I always take in a couple of boarders from out of town. I'll be too busy to squeeze you in."

"I'll take my chances with the pink rods. Just get rolling Effie," she said. She picked up a packet of end papers and handed me one, real impatient.

Fine, I thought, if she's in such an all-fired hurry, I'll just shut my mouth and roll! I didn't say a word for a long time. Then, while I was squirting on the perm solution, just to make small talk I said, "You think Marv'll recognize you with this new look you're going to have?"

That's all I said, but she jerked like I'd dropped hot grease on her. Her face got pink, then red, then almost purple, and she said, "I don't care what that man thinks of my hair!" Then she looked at herself in the mirror and started bawling like a lost calf. Before I could get her a Kleenex, she wiped her nose on the drape she was wearing, which didn't make me any too happy. I only have three of them, and I don't do laundry until Monday.

Before I could say, "Sorry I asked!" she ripped off that drape, threw it on the floor, grabbed her big old paisley handbag and ran into the back room. The front door opened, and Sheriff Tate walked in wearing those nasty one-way sunglasses he always has on. "Say," he said, "Imogene Banks hasn't been by here this afternoon has she?"

"She's back there in the bathroom right now."

We waited, must have been ten minutes, and finally we went back and knocked on the door. When there was no answer, he kicked the door open. Of course the bathroom was empty. Imogene had ducked out the back door.

Sheriff Tate gave me a dirty look over the top of his glasses—like it was my fault she wasn't back there. "You call me if you get any information as to her whereabouts!" he said, and he stomped out of the shop and got into his patrol car. He burned rubber pulling away from the curb, and he squealed around the corner at Main and Webster, probably headed out toward Imogene's house, the one place she for sure wouldn't be.

I put Imogene's drape in the hamper, but I wasn't sure what to do with the neutralizing solution for her perm. It looked like she wouldn't be coming back, but I didn't want to waste it. I set it on the shelf with the other perm supplies and started putting the rods away. Then it hit me. Imogene had left here wearing every single last one of my pink rods! I figured I could make it through my evening appointments with the reds, blues and grays, but I would definitely need the pinks on Saturday. I did not like the idea of canceling my Saturday morning appointments to drive up to Grand Island to buy some more. It wasn't right. What would make a person do something like that?

Linda Lou Phillips — Friday

In spite of what you may have heard over at Effie Cunningham's beauty shop, I want to say right now that I am not responsible for the Imogene Banks mess. If anybody's to blame, it's the wind.

It was blowing like crazy when my sister called this morning and asked me to come into town to cover for her down at the Willa Cather Pioneer Memorial. I was more than glad to do it. Buddy had already taken Buddy Jr. to school, and it was spooky being out there by myself with the wind whistling around the corners like someone trying to get in. I touched up my hair with my curling iron and drove on into town

Of course it wasn't just the wind that brought on the trouble. You could also blame it on Willa Cather. If I hadn't read that story, the whole thing wouldn't have happened, but there was nobody in the bookstore and nothing to do, so—even though I knew from high school that her books are boring—I started reading one of her short stories. It started out slow, but around the middle there was a part that really got me, about this town girl who'd gotten married and moved to a farm, and she's about to go crazy out there, but her father-in-law's really nice and washes the dishes for her so she and her husband can go into town to a movie. I never thought I'd get choked up over a Willa Cather story, but I did, and I read the whole thing without putting it down, even though it was a really long short story.

Right as I finished it, the sun came out, and it was like spring had arrived in Red Cloud at that moment. I was too worked up to stay inside and dust books, so I pulled a chair outside and just sat there on Webster Street, letting my hair blow against my cheek and soaking up the sunshine and thinking about the people in that story. Suddenly, a voice right beside me said, "Hold onto your bonnet!" It was Marv Banks, grinning and holding onto his cowboy hat.

He asked me if I'd had lunch yet, and when I said no, he invited me to join him for the buffet over at the Elavoni. It sounded a lot better than the meatloaf sandwich I'd brought, and there wasn't a car in sight on Webster Street, so I went in and got my purse and locked the front door.

The wind picked up as we walked over to the Elavoni, and just as Marv opened the door for me, a big old gust practically knocked me over. I grabbed Marv's arm just to keep from falling backwards, and I guess that's what Rose saw when she looked up to see who was coming in—me holding onto Marv.

She came right over to take our order. She looked like she'd been out in the wind herself—her frizzy gray hair was sticking out every which way. Marv told her we were both having the buffet, and she brought us each a plate hot from the dishwasher and stood there watching us through those thick glasses of hers. What in the world was she hoping to see? Marv's a nice-looking man, but he's old enough to be my father.

The buffet had all my favorites: corn meal muffins, macaroni and cheese, three-bean salad, and barbequed ribs. When we got back to the table, Marv asked me, "What's the matter with your eye?"

"I don't know. Something from the wind."

He asked if I wanted him to take a look at it, and I said sure. We bent toward each other so he could look into my eye.

He twirled the corner of his handkerchief into a point. "Now, don't move," he said. As he leaned toward me, so intent on helping me out, I thought, He's sweet, like the father-in-law in the story.

That's when the tomato hit the window.

"Get down!" Marv yelled, but before I could move—splat!—a second one hit the glass. Between the two red splatters I saw Imogene Banks with a plaid shopping bag over her arm. She pointed her finger first at Marv, then at me. Her lips were moving, but I couldn't make out a single word she was saying.

Marv got her message, though, and said, "Oh, bad timing."

Then Imogene stuck her hand down into that shopping bag again and pulled out a can of Campbell's cream of mushroom soup. Rose yelled, "Stop her, Marvin, for God's sake! She's going to bust that window!" but before he could get up, Imogene heaved that can straight at us. Sure enough, it broke the window, but fortunately only one piece of glass came out, and it just bounced off of Marv's shoulder and onto the floor.

Imogene went and jumped into that old gray truck that she always has to drive because Marv takes their new red Camaro to work. She started it up, ground the gears into reverse, and was out of there before Marv could get to the door.

"Sorry," Marv said, and he took off.

"Not half as sorry as you're going to be," Rose yelled after him.

She came over to check out the damage to the window, and then she asked me if I wanted to box up the rest of my lunch and take it with me.

"Sorry, Rose," I said. "I don't think I have enough money to cover it."

"Don't worry," she said and went and taped the check to the top of the cash register. "He'll pay."

Imogene Banks — Friday

I stopped by the nursing home this morning to see Marv's mother after I finished the grocery shopping in town. Even though her hip isn't nearly healed up, Mama Banks said she cannot bear to stay in the nursing home another week. She doesn't want to go home, though, and have a nurse take care of her there. "That's for people who don't have kin," she said. "I'm moving in with you and Marv."

I didn't want to go home and brood about it all alone and have it ruin our anniversary, so I went looking for Marv. When the guys at the Farmer's Exchange told me he'd gone out to lunch, I walked on over to the Elavoni. He was there all right, nuzzling up to Linda Lou Phillips right there in the front window, for me and the whole world to see. I probably would have shot him if I'd had a gun, but he keeps the rifle in the Camaro now, so I just threw most of our anniversary dinner at him.

When I got home, I went in the back door and set the shopping bag down on the counter gently so as not to bruise the rest of the tomatoes. It was warm in the kitchen, so I went into my sewing room, where it was cool, and sat down at the machine.

Then I heard Marv's boots on the front steps. He was bellowing, "Imogene! Imogene!"

He burst into the sewing room and said exactly what I knew he was going to say: "Honey, it wasn't what it looked like!" His voice sounded strange to me, like it was coming from inside a barrel. His lips looked like big pink worms, wriggling around his words: "You've got to trust me, Hon! You know there's no one but you!"

I turned back to the window and sat there staring at the dirt road that leads to the highway, remembering all the other times he'd told me it wasn't what it looked like. Finally he said, "Aw, meet me back in town after I get off work. We can have dinner at the steak house and talk this through." He waited for me to say something, but I didn't.

"Well, I got to get back," he said. He came over like he was going to kiss me, but when he got up close, he changed his mind and patted my shoulder. Then he took off for work.

I decided to sew a few more bunny pinafores before I headed back into town for my three o'clock appointment with Effie down at the beauty shop. I wanted to have at least three dozen bunnies ready for the craft show tomorrow when all those Cather people get out of their sessions.

I started feeling better as soon as I turned on the sewing machine. Before I could really get going, though, the phone rang. It was Marv's son, Roger. He said his pickup had broken down, and he had to borrow the truck for a couple of weeks. Last time he borrowed it for a couple of weeks, I was stuck out there for three months without transportation.

I saw what was coming: Mama Banks moving into my sewing room, lock, stock, and barrel. Roger taking my truck away indefinitely, and me waiting on that mean old woman twenty-four hours a day while Marvin carried on his monkey business in town.

All of a sudden I knew I wouldn't be going back to that house after my hair appointment. I started tossing things into a suitcase. I pulled out my underwear drawer and dumped the whole thing in, and there on the bottom was the aqua teddy that Marv got me for our anniversary the year before last. It brought me up short, but then I remembered him staring into Linda Lou Phillips' eyes in the Elavoni, and I kept packing.

The teddy got me thinking about the valentine shorts I bought for him last year. I really didn't want him wearing them with Linda Lou. It kept eating at me, so after I finished packing, I went through his underwear drawer, but they weren't there. They weren't in his pajama drawer or his sweater drawer either. His bottom drawer was stuffed with things like hunting gloves and zip-off hoods for parkas he doesn't have anymore, but I pawed through it anyway, just in case they were in there. At the back was a big square box covered with cellophane. I pulled it out. It was a jumbo pack of Trojans, extra sensitive, and it had been opened.

I set the box on top of the dresser and counted the foil packets.

Eight of the twenty-four were missing. I'd heard about Trojans ever since junior high school, but I'd never seen one before, so I opened one up and unrolled it. It was real slippery. Just like Marv.

I am not proud of what I did next. I felt the shears in my hand. Then I was standing in front of Marv's side of the closet, and then pant legs were flying every which way. Levi legs hit the walls and ceiling. Two brown corduroy legs fell side by side on the bed. A tan leg from his favorite western-cut suit draped itself over the lampshade like someone had put it there on purpose.

Then in the back of my mind I heard a voice say, "Put down the shears, Imogene. Get your stuff and leave."

I went into my sewing room and tried to pull my sewing machine toward the door, but that big old cabinet was too heavy for me, even on rollers. It had been my mama's machine, and I surely hated to leave it behind. Couldn't be helped, though.

I picked up my sewing box, went into the bedroom to gather up some bedding, and swung by the kitchen to grab my shopping bag.

While I was stuffing all that into the cab of the truck, I remembered money. The only money I have is what I've made from selling my crafts, around six hundred dollars in fives and ones, pressed in the pages of my Willa Cather novels. I went back in and got all twelve books, and then I headed out the dirt road to the highway.

I made it to Effie's on time, but before she could finish my perm, the sheriff showed up, and I had to get out of there quick. Rose must have sent him after me because of the window, or maybe Marvin went home early and found his pants. I knew they'd all be on the lookout for the truck, so I drove to the edge of town and backed in between two road graders in the heavy equipment shed that's run by the county.

I found a wooden box and dragged it over to where the light was good. I sat there trying to finish up bunny pinafores by hand until the light got dim. As soon as I stopped sewing, I started remembering everything that had happened since I got up this morning, and it made my head spin.

I climbed into the cab of the truck, pulled some blankets around me, and locked both doors. When I lay down, the rods dug into my scalp, and the chemicals from the perm made my eyes burn, but I was so tired I could have slept anyway if it hadn't been for the howling. It was the weirdest sound I'd ever heard—and it was coming out of me.

Jeanette Pierce — Friday

There's a woman asleep on my floor, and I don't even know her name.

I was having a hard time even before she showed up. I'd spent a disturbing afternoon with Willa Cather down at the archives. In some of her letters, she wasn't just outspoken—she was cruel. And her theatre reviews were so vicious that she was known as "the meat ax critic." It seemed that the more I found out about her, the less I liked her, and I began to wonder whether I could bear to spend the next three years writing my dissertation on her.

I was in such a bad mood by evening that I skipped the Welcome Barbeque and ate trail mix in my room. Around nine I gave up on revising my research outline and called Vivien.

"Keep your eye on the prize, Babe," she said when I told her my doubts about Willa Cather. "Don't let Willa bring you down. Write, Jeanette, write. The cats miss you. I do too. Hurry home and clean the cat box."

When I finally went to bed, I couldn't sleep. I was extremely irritated with Vivien for talking me into coming to this conference in Red Cloud. She thought the excitement of it might loosen my writer's block and speed me toward my Ph.D. Ever since she got tenure at Stanford, she's been pushing me to finish. She can't wait to present us as Dr. and Dr. instead of Dr. and Mrs.

I tossed and turned and deeply regretted choosing community housing for my stay at the conference. Of course I couldn't have known ahead of time that I would be assigned to stay with Effie Cunningham, owner of the Cut and Curl Beauty Shop.

My room smelled of ammonia because the beauty shop adjoined my room, so I got up and opened a window. Just as I was drifting off, someone in the beauty shop yelled, "All right, cut it off. Cut it all off."

Effie, said, "Honey, I don't know what else we can do. Your hair is completely fried. There is no way to restore it."

There was a pitiful moaning sound, and Effie said, "You're going to have to stop that right now. I have a couple from Kansas City in one bedroom and a gal from San Francisco in the other, and you're going to wake them up if you don't pipe down right now."

The noise stopped, and after a while Effie said, "All right. This is what we have to work with. What do you want me to do? I could feather the bangs and try for a pixie look."

"No. Give me that cut Willa Cather had when she left Red Cloud. You know, like in the picture down at the Memorial."

"You mean that crew cut?"

"Yeah. That's it."

It was quiet for a while, and then a door slammed, and the voices stopped. A couple of minutes later, I heard a rhythmic squeaking in the back yard. I looked out my window and saw a stocky woman with very short hair sitting in a swing, moving gently to and fro. It went on and on until finally I put on my bathrobe and slippers and went out the back door. I crossed the damp lawn and sat down in the swing next to hers.

"I'm staying in that room over there with the open window, and your swing is really squeaky," I said. "Would you mind waiting until tomorrow morning to swing?"

"Oh, I'm sorry," she said and stopped swinging. We sat there in the silence. The air smelled of plowed earth and spring, and above the swing set, a crab apple tree was in bloom.

She turned to me and asked what I'd do with a man who gave me an aqua-colored teddy and then turned around and cheated on me with other women.

"Shoot him," I said.

"I wanted to this morning," she said, "but now I don't know." She told me how he'd found the teddy at Victoria's Secret in Grand Island and had them send to the main factory to get just that color in an extra large. "You don't find a man like that every day," she said.

"What is a teddy anyway?" I asked her. "I've never had one."

"The crotch snaps," she said. "Otherwise it's just like a camisole."

She ran her hand across her hair, and her lower lip started to tremble.

"Nice haircut," I told her. "Effie did a good job."

She covered her face with her hands.

"Really—it's bold," I said, but I could see it didn't help.

After a couple of minutes, she pulled herself together and asked me to give her a ride to her truck, which was parked at the heavy equipment shed just south of town. She didn't seem dangerous, and she had quit swinging for my sake, so I went in and got the keys to my rental car and drove her there.

It took all of three minutes. She opened her door and got out. The shed was huge and dark and smelled of diesel fumes and rust.

I knew the smart thing to do was to say "Good luck," and drive straight back to Effie's place and put in my earplugs, but I couldn't stop myself from asking, "What are you going to do now?"

"Sleep in my truck. Thanks for the lift." She walked off into the darkness.

"Wait. Do you want to come back and stay with me at Effie's?"

The crunch of her footsteps in the gravel stopped. "All right. Just a minute."

A couple of minutes later she came back carrying a huge armload of sheets and blankets all wadded together. She had a book under her arm. "Look," she said when she got into the car. I turned on the overhead light. It was a hardbound copy of *My Antonia*. I opened it and read, "To the Lindstroms, who know all about life on the Divide. Regards, Willa Cather. 1918."

"What a great thing to have!"

"My grandmother had her sign it. She wasn't afraid of her like a lot of people were."

"Does it bother you that Willa Cather wasn't a nice person?"

"Nice? I spent my whole life being nice. I think Willa Cather had the right idea."

When we got back to my room at the Cut and Curl, she made a nest of blankets on the floor and crawled into it. I thought she was asleep, but suddenly she sat up and looked out the window. Then she turned to me and said, "The sheriff is after me. But don't worry. It isn't what it sounds like."

Then she did go to sleep—but I didn't.

Effie — Saturday

This has been quite a day already, and it isn't even noon yet!

I told everyone when they arrived yesterday that I would

serve breakfast at 7:30 sharp today. I didn't feel like getting up early, but I did, and I got bacon, eggs, and hash browns on the table by 7:30. Nobody showed up. I waited five minutes, and then I went to call them.

Well, the couple from Kansas City, when I got to their door, it was clear what they were doing and that they weren't going to be out for awhile.

I went and tapped on the door of the gal from San Francisco.

"Yes?"

"Breakfast's on the table!"

"Oh, thanks, I'll be there in a minute."

Now, if I'd gone right back to the kitchen, that would have been the end of it, but I saw some mud on the carpet in front of her door. Somebody must have tracked it in last night, which didn't make me any too happy, but I got a sponge from the bathroom and got down on my hands and knees and scrubbed it up. Just as I was standing up to leave, I heard the sound of voices whispering inside her room.

I would not have pegged this gal as somebody who would be sneaking a man into her room in the middle of the night. Who could she have found at such short notice? Not many men come to these things, and the ones who do seem kind of reserved. I thought maybe she'd picked somebody up down at the bar. I sure hoped it wasn't Marv Banks!

I went back to the kitchen. While I was putting Saran Wrap over the bacon and eggs to keep the flies off of them, I heard the side door slam. Yep, it was her, and she was getting into her car with someone I couldn't really see very well, someone who was wearing a raincoat and dark glasses and a scarf. Something about the scarf looked awfully familiar. I got up closer to the window to get a better look, and sure enough, it was my dresser scarf, the hand-embroidered one I bought at the craft sale last Christmas!

I decided then and there if that scarf was not back on the dresser by Sunday morning, I was going to charge her for it.

Hmm! I thought. So it was a woman in here with her last night. Could be just a friend. I hoped that was it.

I was a little suspicious, though. You know, since those rumors have been going around that Willa Cather was a—you know—it seems like more and more of these gals with short, blunt haircuts have been coming to the conferences.

Now, I didn't want to jump to conclusions about the gal's personal life. It's really none of my business, but the situation had created a problem for me. My rates for the conference are twenty-five dollars a night for one person and thirty-five dollars a night for two. I think that's quite reasonable, especially with a complete breakfast included. I really didn't think I could let her get away with paying that lower rate with two people in the room, but how was I going to bring it up?

I didn't have much time to stew about it. The couple from Kansas City showed up, hungry as bears. By the time I got them fed and got the kitchen cleaned up, it was time to go into my shop and get set up for my 10:00 appointment.

I was sweeping up Imogene Banks' hair from last night when I heard a car door slam. I took a look, and sure enough, it was the San Francisco gal back again. The passenger door opened, and out came a man in a dark suit and hat. The side door slammed, and I heard them go into her room and close the door.

This was too much for me. Last night a woman in her room. Now a man. What kind of place did she think I was running here? I marched down the hall and knocked on her door.

"Who is it?"

"Effie," I said, and I opened the door and walked right in.

The man had taken off his hat and jacket and was sitting in the armchair by the window. He was all lit up from behind by the sun, and at first I couldn't see what he was doing. It looked almost like he was threading a needle.

"Effie," he said, "I know what I need to do next!"

It wasn't a man at all. It was Imogene Banks, and she had a lapful of those hand-sewed bunnies with pinafores that she always sells at the craft shows.

"I'm going to leave Red Cloud and make my living by sewing like Lena Lingard did," she said.

"Like who?"

"Lena Lingard—you know, in *My Antonia*

I nodded. I had heard of the book.

I turned to the San Francisco gal and said, "I suppose this was your idea."

"No," Imogene said. "My mama told me to do it just as I was waking up this morning."

"Honey, your mama's been dead for sixteen years."

"That's true," said Imogene, "but she's helping me from the other side."

Well, I don't usually put much stock in the other side, but Imogene looked so much better than she had a few hours before, I was willing to believe she was getting help from somewhere. I asked her, "What did she tell you to do?"

"I was in that state between sleep and waking up, and I heard Mama's voice say, 'It's time to move on, Honey.'

" 'All right,' I said. 'Where should I go and what should I do?' She didn't say anything, but I heard the sound of a sewing machine in the background."

Meanwhile, the San Francisco gal was lying on the bed with a pillow behind her head, trying to keep her eyes open. "Where do you fit into all this?" I asked her.

She looked at me kind of stunned. "I wish I knew!" she said, and then her eyes closed and stayed that way.

"She's helped me a lot," said Imogene. "Let me sleep on the floor here last night, took me to get these clothes this morning."

"Where did you get that suit?"

"At the nursing home. It's been hanging in the closet of Mama Banks' room ever since she got there. It belonged to the old guy who was there before her, and nobody claimed it when he died. I knew Mama Banks would be sleeping early this morning, so I just slipped in, put it on, and walked out. Do you think it's a good disguise?"

"You fooled me—and the price was right," I told her. "Now what's the plan?"

"Plan?" she said, and I saw that even with help from the other side, I was going to have my hands full.

Linda Lou Phillips — Saturday

My nails are ruined—but it was worth it.

Every year the P.E.O. puts on a salad luncheon for the Cather Conference, and it's one of my favorite events. This morning, though, when I arrived at the luncheon, several of my P.E.O. sisters gave me the cold shoulder. I couldn't understand why they were snubbing me. Then when I went into the kitchen with my rhubarb pie, someone said in a loud whisper, "Hang on to your husband—here she comes!"

I held my head up high and walked right past them, but my face was burning. It must be all over town about Imogene Banks and those tomatoes. While I was slicing the pie, I realized I had to fix this up fast. The P.E.O. elections are next week, and I'm running for president.

Then it came to me. I made two rhubarb pies this morning. I could take the extra one out to Imogene Banks after the luncheon and explain that absolutely nothing is going on between me and her husband.

I was a little nervous on the drive out there. When I turned into their driveway, I saw Imogene's truck parked all by itself in front of the house. I took a deep breath, got out of my car, got the pie, and headed for the porch.

Then as I started up the steps, who should come out the front door but Effie Cunningham. She had her hair up in rollers, like she always does, but she was puffing and sweating, which I have never seen her do before. She held the screen door open with her hip while she tried to pull something out the door. "One, two, three, push!" she said, and out rolled Imogene's sewing machine. Some woman I didn't recognize was pushing it from behind. She looked like one of those women from the Cather conference: elastic-waist pants, bifocals, gray hair. She had one of those short, straight haircuts.

Then Effie saw me. "Good," she said. "You can help us load this into the truck."

The Cather woman and I pushed from the back and Effie guided the front. Just as we got it onto the boards that were propped between the porch and the truck bed, Marv's red Camaro came roaring down the driveway and stopped in a cloud of dust right behind my car. Marv jumped out one side, and his son Roger jumped out the other. It was a cool day, but Marv was wearing cut-offs.

"What the hell is going on here?" he said.

"Imogene wants her sewing machine," Effie told him.

"You're not taking that machine or the truck either. Imogene can just get herself home here where she belongs."

Marv and Effie stood there glaring at each other. Then something strange happened. The boards under the sewing machine creaked, and we all looked over there. Nobody was standing anywhere near it. All by itself, that heavy old Singer sewing machine started rolling toward the truck. It speeded up and rolled right off the boards and stopped dead center in the truck bed.

"Well, I guess that's it then," Effie said. She shoved the boards into the truck and told me to put up the tailgate. Marv just stood there staring at the sewing machine. He was real pale.

The nails I hadn't wrecked on the sewing machine were destroyed when I hooked up the tailgate, but I kept a smile on my face and told Effie as she got into the truck, "Be sure to tell Imogene 'hi' from me. Oh, and give her this!" I ran and got the pie from the edge of the porch and passed it in the window to her.

Marv came over to me after they drove away. "I was sort of hoping that pie was for me," he said and gave me a big wink. I've got to hand to him. The man never gives up.

Marv and Roger went inside, and I came on home to get supper on for Buddy Junior and re-do my nails before the banquet. Imogene is supposed to get an award tonight. I hope she shows up. I'll make sure Buddy Senior and I sit right beside her.

Imogene — Saturday

Effie came bustling into the house with Jeanette, the gal from San Francisco, right behind her. Jeanette handed me a rhubarb pie and said she was going to her room to take a nap. Effie told me that it's all over town that I'm going to get an award at the banquet tonight, and I'd better go.

"I can't go," I told her. "Sheriff Tate's sure to be there."

"You need the money," she said.

"What money? It's just a certificate that says, 'Volunteer of the Year.'"

"Not this year. Rose says they're giving you a $250 gift certificate from the Wal-Mart in Grand Island."

I started thinking of all the things I could buy with that. One of those squeegee things to clean bugs off the windshield of the truck. Windex. Paper towels. An ice chest and a tape recorder and some Emmy Lou Harris tapes. Everything I need for my trip and my new life.

Effie said I should go to the banquet incognito. She said people wouldn't recognize me in my suit and hat if I didn't talk to anybody. I said maybe I could do that if she could stick right by me all night, but she has to help serve the meal. I was about to give it up, when Effie got an idea. "Why don't you go with Jeanette?"

Effie went into her shop, and I went into the kitchen and cut myself a piece of pie. I took a bite, and it was the best rhubarb pie I'd ever tasted. I cut a piece for Jeanette and went to her room.

She didn't wake up when I came in, so I just sat in the armchair and ate my pie and looked out the window. It was getting on toward evening. The clouds were turning dark pink, almost red, and the crab apple blossoms looked so pretty against the sky, I thought, "How can I leave this place?"

Then Jeanette woke up and I handed her the pie. She sat up in bed and ate it.

"Mmm," she said. "That's good."

"Fresh rhubarb. You probably don't get that very often in the city."

"No," she said.

"But it's nice there?"

"Oh, yes."

"Well, I've been thinking. Lena Lingard started out as a dressmaker in Lincoln, but later on Tiny Soderball talked her into moving to San Francisco. Maybe at my age I'll skip Lincoln and go straight to San Francisco."

She smiled and kept on eating her pie.

I asked her if she had plans to go to the banquet with anybody.

She said that the only people she'd met since she came to Red Cloud were Effie, me, Linda Lou, Marv, and Roger.

"Well," I told her, "Effie has to help serve the meal, so it sounds to me like I'm your best bet! You want to go with me?"

"I'd love to," she said.

When I looked at myself in the mirror, I had no idea who that was, but whoever it was was looking downright bold.

Jeanette Pierce — Saturday

I skipped all the conference presentations on Saturday because I was busy helping Imogene and Effie. I didn't mind—I wouldn't have missed it for anything.

I wasn't planning to go to the banquet until Imogene invited me to go with her. Since she was all dressed up in her suit and hat from the nursing home, I put on a fancy dress—my only dress—and some dangly earrings, and off we went to the high school gymnasium.

Effie was in the serving line behind a steam table of mashed potatoes. She pulled us aside and told Imogene not to say a word till she had the gift certificate in her hand. She told her to have her keys in the other hand, and if Sheriff Tate caused any trouble, she should duck out the fire exit and just start driving. She didn't need to worry about him following her—Effie's nephew had already let the air out of his tires.

Imogene located Sheriff Tate, and we sat as far away from him as possible at a table with some Cather people.

Once dessert and coffee were served, the director of the Willa Cather Pioneer Memorial stepped up to the podium. "While you're enjoying your pineapple upside down cake, we want to thank some folks who have made special contributions to the WCPM this year." I reached over and squeezed Imogene's hand.

The director said, "We have a special award this time for our Volunteer of the Year. Unfortunately, it doesn't look like our winner, Imogene Banks, is here tonight."

Imogene rose and walked to the podium. The director stepped back and glanced around uncomfortably. Imogene held out her hand for the award. The director hid it behind her back. Imogene didn't move, just stood there with her hand out.

Then Effie came up to the podium, carrying a pot of coffee. "It's Imogene all right. I gave her that haircut myself. Now you give her the gift certificate."

A buzz went through the crowd. The Cather people were saying, "Who's Imogene?" and the locals were saying, "That's Imogene?"

The director handed over the award. Imogene stepped up to the podium. "Thanks for this, and for everything we've shared since I came to Red Cloud. No matter where I end up, I'm going to miss all of you."

While everyone was still applauding, Imogene started toward her seat, but Effie grabbed her arm and pulled her back to the front. Effie said, "Are we going to let Imogene drive out of here with nothing but a blue tarp to cover her mama's sewing machine in the back of her truck? It's her only means of supporting herself. I think we ought to take up a collection to buy her a camper shell!"

A lot of people nodded agreement, but one woman stood up and said, "She has no business leaving her mother-in-law with no one to take care of her." Several other people at that table nodded and said, "That's right."

I'm usually reticent in large groups, but those people made me so angry that I stood up and said, "I admire Imogene for heading off into the unknown with nothing but a truck and a sewing machine. It seems to me she's a perfect example of the pioneer spirit we celebrate in the work of Willa Cather. I'd like to donate $60."

Well, that did it. Purses were opened; wallets were pulled out of back pockets. Effie collected the donations in her apron and presented them to Imogene, who stuffed the bills in her jacket pockets and the change in her pants pockets. She gave the crowd a huge smile.

After the banquet, Imogene and I got back to the Cut and Curl first, but Effie was right behind us. She put on a pot of coffee, and the three of us sat at the kitchen table reliving the best moments of the banquet and finishing off the rhubarb pie. We counted Imogene's money—four hundred and eighty dollars—and Effie said it would be more than enough to buy a used camper shell for the truck. She also said my speech was grand.

"Don't go to bed," I told them, and I went to the liquor store for a bottle of champagne. When I got back, we toasted Imogene's new life. While we shared a few more rounds, Effie and Imogene told me long and winding stories about Linda Lou Phillips and Marv and Roger and Rose and the Director of the Willa Cather Pioneer Memorial.

When we finished the champagne, Effie brewed another pot of coffee. Then she and Imogene told me stories of Willa Cather, how she sent food to Red Cloud during the Depression, how she had a fit when some businessmen cut down the cottonwood trees on Main Street, how some people in Red Cloud loved her and others hated her, but none of them could avoid belonging to her because she had folded their lives into her books and sent them singing out into the wide world.

Effie was a master storyteller, and Imogene was no slouch. I wanted them to go on and on. As I listened to their stories, a passage from My *Antonia* came into my mind. I found it in Imogene's copy: "Although I admired scholarship so much in Cleric, I was not deceived about myself; I knew that I should never be a scholar. I could never lose myself for long among impersonal things. Mental excitement was apt to send me with a rush back to my own naked land and the figures scattered upon it."

I got goose bumps as I read Willa's words. Eighty-four years ago she'd captured the truth about me. I wanted to write stories, not dissertations about stories, and that was all there was to it. That was what I'd come to Red Cloud to learn.

"Effie," I said, "Would you cut my hair?"

"Now?" she asked.

"Yes," I said, and she led the way to the beauty shop. I sat down in the chair, and Imogene leaned against the counter. Effie unfolded a drape with a snap of her wrist, wrapped it around my shoulders, and secured the Velcro fastener at my throat.

"How do you want it?" she asked.

I knew I wanted to look different, but I didn't have an image in mind. I was drunk, but not drunk enough to give Effie free rein. I turned to Imogene for help, and there was my answer, plain as day.

"Give me that cut Willa Cather had when she left Red Cloud," I said.

Effie narrowed her eyes. "You're not going to regret this in the morning, are you?"

"I hope not," I said, and Effie picked up her scissors and cut off all my hair. She used electric clippers to do the sides and back.

"How much do I owe you?" I asked as she whisked the short hairs off me.

"Standard. Twenty-five," she said, and I paid her.

"I'm going to bed," she said.

"I'm going out to look at the stars," I said and went out the back door. Imogene came out too.

The stars were hanging low and bright like they never do in the city.

"You take the squeaky one this time," Imogene said, and I did. We both pushed off and then pumped higher and higher. It sounded awful, but I kept going because all around my naked head I felt the winds of freedom blowing. From the way Imogene was laughing, I was fairly sure she felt them too.

First Date

I was dead tired when I got home from work, but Barbara met me at the door and said she needed me to pick Ben up from his play date with Alexander. It was the last thing in the world I felt like doing, but I said all right because I knew if I refused, I'd have to listen to everything she'd done all day and all she still had to do. She gave me a slip of paper with an address. I said, "I thought they lived in Noe Valley," and she said, "No, you're thinking of Alexander B. He lives in Noe Valley, but Alexander P. lives in Bernal Heights."

I drove to Bernal Heights, feeling grouchy about how play dates suck up so much time. Barbara said we've got to do them, though, because if kids don't have play dates, and the other kids start talking about *their* play dates, the ones without play dates feel like rejects.

"Hey," I said to her, "isn't there enough time for that in high school?"

I found the address and parked and went up and rang the bell. I felt stupid standing there and not knowing who was going to answer the door. It was like being on a blind date.

A tall gal in Nike running shorts opened the door and said, "You must be Ben's dad. I'm Joanne." Her hair was short, and her handshake was firm, I mean *firm*. I've noticed that in San Francisco. The women tend to have extremely firm handshakes. I squeezed back hard, to let her know I wasn't intimidated, and we went into the living room, where another woman was sitting on the sofa eating pistachios. This one was all curves and dimples. She didn't stand up, just licked the salt off her fingers and said, "Hi, I'm Eileen. Want some pistachios?"

"No thanks," I said. I was really hungry, but I didn't feel like cracking pistachio shells with my teeth in front of people I didn't know.

"The kids are downstairs," Eileen said. "I'll go get them." She got up, stepped over a puzzle of Noah's ark, and put her bare foot down on something sharp. She yelped and picked up an action figure of Batman and threw it across the room.

It wasn't exactly surprising that she'd stepped on a toy—there wasn't a square foot of carpet that didn't have trains or blocks or stuffed animals or puzzles or kids' clothes on it. Seemed to me like maybe Joanne had been out jogging when she should have been cleaning. Barbara never lets our living room get into that kind of shape. Even when she had to have a C-section with Ben, she was up cleaning the day after she got home from the hospital.

Right after Eileen went downstairs, there were heavy footsteps on the front stairs, and the doorbell rang. "That must be Ron," Joanne said and opened the door.

A muscular guy with an expensive haircut came in carrying a roaster pan with the lid on. "This is Ben's dad," Joanne told him.

"Chuck," I said and put out my hand. Ron set the pan down,

but before we could shake, Alexander came running in and jumped up into Ron's arms. "Daddy!" he said.

Then my son Ben came around the corner wearing a blue dress-looking thing. I'd be lying if I said it didn't bother me. This had come up before, back in Colorado. He'd had on a pink tutu one afternoon when I went to pick him up at preschool. His teacher told me it was normal, and a couple of times after that I noticed that the class bully—a big bruiser—was wearing the tutu while he terrorized the other kids, so I stopped worrying about Ben wearing it. But now I figured Ben was old enough to know better.

"What do you have on?" I asked him.

"Oh, Alexander's cousin donated that to the costume box," Joanne said.

"I don't want to go home!" Ben said.

"Come on, Sport, Mommy's waiting," I told him.

From his father's arms, Alexander said to Ben, "You can't take the Tinker Bell nightgown home."

"I know that," Ben said and stripped it off and threw it on the floor. I was way glad to see that he had on his underwear. Joanne went and got his jeans and T-shirt and shoes and handed them to me, so I started dressing him. It wasn't that easy, but she didn't offer to help, even though he'd taken his clothes off in her house.

Ron took the roasting pan into the kitchen, and I could hear him banging around in there. It was unclear to me who to say thanks to for the play date, so I just tossed it over my shoulder and headed for the door with Ben. I was reaching for the doorknob when Ben wailed, "I forgot Clarence!" That's the little orange stuffed armadillo that he has to have to go to sleep. We couldn't leave without Clarence—Barbara would send me back in a minute if we went home without him.

"Where'd you leave him, Hon?" Joanne asked Ben, but he just gave her that same look he always gives me when I ask him what he did in kindergarten that day, like how would he know what happened millions of years ago?

"We had him downstairs," Alexander said, so all four of the adults followed the kids to the basement. Man, I thought the living room was a mess, but the downstairs made it look good. We all started pawing through piles of Legos and Lincoln Logs and Tinker Toys, but no luck.

After awhile it seemed like everybody was losing interest, so I said, "Sorry to put you through this, but he really can't go to sleep without Clarence."

They nodded, but I could tell they were getting irritated. Ron asked Alexander, "Are you *sure* you left him down here?" Alexander shrugged.

"All right, we'd better be systematic about this," Ron said. "How about two of us continue down here, and two of us take the upstairs?"

I headed upstairs, toward the area of lesser chaos. I hoped Eileen would come upstairs too, but she and Joanne continued to sort through the wreckage below, and Ron followed me up.

"You want something to drink?" he asked me. "I think they have Coke and root beer in the fridge."

"Sure," I said, and we went into the kitchen, opened a couple of root beers, and started our search.

I hadn't drunk root beer since high school, and the taste took me back to hot summer afternoons at the A&W Root Beer stand out on south Townsend. It was right next to the swimming pool, and I spent three months drinking root beer from frosty mugs and trying to get up enough nerve to ask out one of the lifeguards. Her name was Carol. When I finally asked her at the end of August, she said no. Right after that, I got together with Barbara, and that's all she wrote.

Joanne didn't seem like the type to wear perfume, but her bedroom smelled good, and there were a bunch of fancy bottles on the dresser. There were satin sheets on the bed, too. I started thinking maybe she had a side to her that wasn't obvious on first meeting. I was about to look into her drawers to see if she wore sexy underwear, but Ron came in and started looking under the bed.

He dusted off his pants when he stood up.

"Dirty down there," he said.

"Yep," I said.

"I know they're busy with Alexander and all, but they could hire somebody to come in once a week," he said.

"Did you use to live here?" I asked.

"Heavens, no!" he said.

"Well, if you don't mind my asking, how come Alexander calls you Daddy?"

"I am his father, but they're the parents. I live in Pacific Heights. Here." He picked up a picture off the dresser. "Here's Alexander over at our place."

In the picture, Alexander was sitting on the front steps of a Victorian between Ron and another guy who looked a lot like Ron. "That's Dave," Ron said. "He's in L.A. this weekend."

OK. So this was a lesbian-moms, gay-guy-dads situation. Did Barbara know that's what she was sending me into? I'd had some awkward play-date pick-ups before, but this was off the graph.

Don't get me wrong. I don't have anything against gay people, and I knew when we moved here I was going to encounter some. I was prepared for that, but I wasn't ready to be alone in a bedroom with one.

I went into the bathroom and closed the door and checked in the cabinet under the sink. I saw something orange behind a bottle of Lysol and got down on my hands and knees to investigate. It wasn't Clarence, just an old T-shirt stiff with Comet cleanser. Someone tapped on the bathroom door, so I tried to jump up, but my feet somehow slipped out from under me, and on the way down my face hit the cabinet.

For a minute I sat there watching whirling lights. Then I noticed the salty, metallic taste of blood in the back of my throat and felt blood trickling from my nose. From the other side of the bathroom door, Ron asked, "Are you all right in there?"

"Yeah," I told him. I got to my feet and grabbed a handful of Kleenex and held them to my nose. The blood soaked through right away, and I didn't know what else to do except open the door and say, "I've got a damn nosebleed."

"You sure do," he said, and took a dark green washcloth off the edge of the tub and handed it to me. "Why don't you sit down?" he said, nodding toward the toilet. "I'll get Joanne."

I wondered what he thought Joanne could do, but I put down the toilet lid and sat down like he'd told me to. I heard some doors slam and then some pounding, and then Joanne came in with a plastic bag full of crushed ice. "You need to hold this on your nose," she said and handed it to me.

She seemed to know what she was doing, so I said, "Are you a nurse, or just an experienced mom?"

"I'm a doctor," she said. "You look pretty pale. Why don't you lie down?"

She moved a pile of laundry to the dresser, and I took off my shoes and lay down on the bed. The blood tasted nasty in my throat, but it was easier to keep the washcloth and ice bag on my nose while I was lying down, so I stayed there. Joanne sat on the edge of the bed and adjusted the ice. Her hand brushed against my face, and I felt sort of turned on and sort of like I wanted to cry.

Ben came running in with Alexander. "I'm hungry. I'm going to have macaroni and cheese with Alexander. OK?"

"Can he?" Alexander asked. "Daddy's cooking Scooby Doo macaronis."

"No," I told them. "Remember, Ben, your cousins are coming over for dinner tonight." I looked at my watch and saw that it was almost six. Barbara's brother and his family were probably already at our house, and I hadn't let Barbara know what was going on.

"We've got to go," I told Ben. I sat up, but I felt dizzy. Joanne said, "You can't go until the bleeding stops," like I didn't have any say in the matter. Ben saw the blood on my face and started whimpering. Joanne said, "He's just got a nosebleed, Ben. He's going to be all right. Why don't you go have Scooby Doos with Alexander?"

The boys took off, and I didn't fight it, even though I knew Barbara would kill me for letting Ben eat right before dinner. What could I do? I was bleeding like a stuck pig. Clarence was lost. Ben and I were stranded in the house of homosexuals, and that's just how it was.

Once I gave up, it was a big relief to lie back and let Ron feed Ben while Joanne watched over me and Eileen kept searching for Clarence. Maybe I was light-headed from blood loss or something. I felt like I was floating.

Then it was like I was floating on my back in a swimming pool. I could smell the chlorine and feel the sun on my face and chest. I sank to the bottom and watched a stream of bubbles rise from my mouth to the bright, glassy surface of the pool. I didn't struggle, just lay there resting against the rough cement on the bottom.

Then there was an explosion of silver above me, and Carol swam down to me with swift strokes. She pulled me up, dragged me out of the pool, and put her warm mouth on mine. Then she blew into my lungs, which made me laugh, but she didn't seem to notice. She blew again and again. I could see she was getting desperate, so I told her I was fine, but she couldn't hear me.

She turned into Joanne. We were the only people at the pool, which seemed odd in the middle of the afternoon. Joanne started crying because I wasn't breathing. "Please," she said. She lay down on top of me, trying to warm me up with her body. I understood then that if I didn't move she'd keep doing these incredible things to bring me back to life. She began to move on top of me, with nothing but our nylon Speedo suits between us.

The real Joanne said, "Mmmm!"

"What?"

"Paella."

I was still half in the dream world, and the word "paella" sounded like something out of a fairy tale. What was it? Some bizarre kind of food? A scene from one of Ben's videos flashed into my mind. This little boy and his big sister fall through a tree into Fairyland, and one of the good fairies tells them, "You must not eat anything while you're here. If you do, you can never leave Fairyland." The girl resists the food they offer her, but the little boy forgets and starts eating everything in sight, so he's stuck there.

"Dinner's ready," Ron called from the kitchen, and Joanne got up and left. I could hear chairs scraping and dishes clattering in the dining room. My stomach was growling, but I didn't feel hungry. All I could think about was getting Ben and getting out of there. I checked the washcloth, and it looked like my nose had stopped bleeding, so I got up, ditched the ice bag and washcloth in the sink in the bathroom, and went into the dining room. "Clarence or no Clarence," I said, "we've got to leave now."

"I can't. I'm eating," Ben said and shoveled a spoonful of neon-yellow noodles into his mouth.

It was too late. Ben had eaten in Fairyland. I stood behind his chair, waiting for him to finish and feeling lousy. Of course I knew that video was just a movie, but you know how sometimes made-up stories have a kernel of truth to them? It was my job to protect Ben, and I'd let him down.

"Would you like to try some paella?" Ron asked. "I brought plenty."

"I'd better not," I said. "Barbara's fixing a big meal at home."

"At least sit down with us till Ben's done," Eileen said. "Have a glass of wine."

The wine was good. Ben wanted a second helping of Scooby Doos, and while he ate, Eileen giggled and filled my wine glass again. Her face was flushed, and I wondered how much she'd already had.

Joanne asked me to pass the paella, and when I picked up the platter, the smell of sausage overpowered me.

"Maybe I will try a little," I said.

It turned out to be one of the best things I've ever eaten. Chicken, shrimp, and sausage, all in one dish, and the sausage wasn't the low-calorie fake stuff that Barbara tries to feed us for breakfast. The meat was embedded in yellow rice that melted in my mouth. I couldn't stop eating. After my third helping, I got Ron's phone number and told him I was going to have Barbara call and get the recipe from him. Of course that made me think of Barbara.

"Wipe that cheese off your chin and let's go, Bud," I said to Ben.

He stuck out his lower lip. "Clarence," he said.

"For Pete's sake, Ben, we turned the house upside down, but nobody could find Clarence," I told him. "You're going to have to sleep with something else tonight."

Ben started shaking his head. Tears ran down his cheeks.

Alexander reached over and patted Ben's shoulder. "You can borrow the Tinker Bell nightgown," he said.

Ben stopped crying and wiped his nose with the back of his hand. Alexander ran downstairs before I could think of a polite way to turn down his offer. A couple of minutes later, he burst back into the dining room, holding something behind his back. "Guess what I found? Clarence! He was under the clown wig in the dress-up box."

The adults were all going "Whoopee!" but Ben just said, "Where's the Tinker Bell dress?" Alexander looked from Joanne to Eileen. "Do I still have to let him borrow it? He's got Clarence back."

"Yes, you do, Honey," Joanne said. "You offered it to him. Don't go back on your word."

She went downstairs and got the nightgown. Ben wanted to put it on right away. I said, "How about when we get home?" but he just went ahead and peeled off his clothes. I put the nightgown over his head and fastened the tiny white button at the back of his neck.

Joanne and Alexander walked us to the door. "What do you say to Alexander?" I asked Ben.

"Can I take the Batman cape too?" he said. Joanne and I laughed, but Alexander didn't.

"Thanks," I told them for Ben.

Outside it had turned cold. As soon as the car warmed up, I turned on the heater and put on a Cat Stevens CD. "Oh very young one, what will you leave us this time?" I sang with Cat as I drove toward home.

"How you doing, Buddy?" I asked over my shoulder, but Ben and Clarence had conked out.

At home, my brother-in-law's car was parked in our driveway. I got out of my car and opened the back door. I wondered if I should change Ben's clothes before anyone saw him, but I knew it would wake him up, so I didn't even try. I stood there looking at him in the blue dress, and I remembered a Christmas pageant from when I was a kid. The church was decorated for Christmas with pine boughs, so it smelled like we were in the woods, and the only light was hundreds of candles burning. All the kids who sang were dressed as angels. I had on wings and a silky white gown, and as I sang, I felt the cool air of the sanctuary all over my body, lifting me up with the music. In the glow from the streetlight, Ben looked the way I felt that night—radiant, other-worldly, lighter than air.

I picked him up and held him for a long time before I took him inside.

Lucky Lady

Though she's looking out the window of the observation car at a rush of pines, Melissa doesn't see the trees. She's wishing she'd told her husband how much Motrin to give their daughter if her summer cold brings on a fever.

"Smile," her sister Clare says. "They'll kick us off the fun train if we're not having fun."

"Sorry," Melissa says.

"Let's have another margarita."

"Not for me," Melissa says, but Clare climbs over her and heads down to the bar anyway and comes back with two margaritas in plastic cups.

"It's your fortieth birthday, and you've got thirty-six hours of freedom. Don't waste it." She puts Melissa's margarita in her hand.

Everything goes black. "Tunnel!" screams a kid in the seat in front of them, and Melissa feels a rush of excitement. As they come out into the evening light, Melissa tastes salt and lime and the tequila she hadn't planned to drink.

Clare nods approvingly.

"All right," Melissa says. "You can carry me to the hotel."

"We'll take a taxi."

"Too expensive," Melissa says, but Clare says, "Don't worry. It's on me. Part of your birthday present."

"You've already spent too much on this trip."

"Hey, we've got coupons—free meals, free drinks, free tokens for the slot machines. We're covered."

"But how did you pay for the rest?"

"I sold something."

"Oh, Clare, not drugs."

"No. I told you I don't mess with that anymore."

"You didn't sell Jamie's record collection, did you?"

"No, Melissa, I didn't. Why would you even ask me that?" Clare turns away from her and stares out the window and drinks alone.

Melissa waits and then says, "Sorry. What did you sell?"

"Twenty minutes to Reno! Twenty minutes till we arrive in Reno!" the conductor yells up the steps to the observation car.

"Something of mine," Clare says. "Let's go get our stuff."

By three a.m., Melissa is tired of playing the slots, even though she still has a half-bucket of nickels. She cashes them in for bills and goes to look for Clare. She spots her wild red hair at a blackjack table. The dealer looks like Clark Gable in *Gone With The Wind*, and Melissa watches Clare flirt with him in her edgy, teasing way.

Melissa sits down, feeling more like Clare's dowdy aunt than her sister. She wishes she hadn't worn her black knit pants with the elastic waist and baggy seat. Clare slides a stack of chips over in front of her, but Melissa shakes her head. "I can't add fast in my head," she whispers.

Clare loses that hand and the next three. She takes all the rest of her chips and bets them on the next hand and wins. "Want to stop and get something to eat?" Melissa asks, but Clare shakes her head and keeps playing until she loses everything.

"You know why I like gambling?" Clare asks as they walk away from the table. "Because while I'm doing it, I can't think about anything except what card is going to come up next. There's no room for anything else."

"How much did you lose?"

Clare shrugs and feels in her jeans pocket and brings out a few wadded bills. "A couple of hundred I guess. But look," she says and reaches into her back pocket. "Coupons! You want to have breakfast?"

In the Prospector Coffee Shop, Melissa orders a plain omelet with wheat toast and coffee. Clare orders dollar-sized pancakes, two eggs over easy, and a Bloody Mary.

"Alcoholic drinks aren't included in the coupon special," the waitress says.

"Fine," Clare tells her. "Bring it right away, would you?"

"What is it you don't want to think about?" Melissa asks.

"What?"

"When you gamble?"

"Oh, credit card debt. Toxic waste. Jamie killing himself."

"I miss him too."

"I don't just miss him!" Clare's voice rises. "I don't want to stay in this goddamn world without him!"

"Shhh!" Melissa says. Clare clamps her mouth shut and glares at her.

Melissa looks around uncomfortably. "It's hard to be with you when you're like this."

"Yeah, well think how bad it is for me. I almost never get away from me."

"He was my brother, too. You're not the only one who lost him. It doesn't give you the right to act like an ass."

The waitress brings Clare's Bloody Mary, and she takes a long drink of it. "It's different for you," she says. "You have a family. I don't have anybody."

"You still have me."

Clare swallows hard and stares at her silverware. She keeps her head down while the waitress brings their plates, and when she looks up, her eyes are bright with tears. Melissa reaches across and takes her hand. Clare squeezes her hand and pulls away to blow her nose into a napkin.

They eat in silence until Clare says, "My eggs. That's what I've been selling."

Melissa looks at the eggs on Clare's plate and raises her eyebrows.

"They give me thirty-five hundred dollars. All I have to do is go into artificial menopause for a month and then take a megablast of a fertility drug and then let them stick a huge needle in me to harvest eggs from my ovaries."

"God!"

"Yeah, it really hurts."

"How many times have you done it?"

Clare grins. "Well, strictly speaking, you're only supposed to do it once, but five different places in the city buy them, so I'm making the rounds."

"Aren't you worried about running out of eggs? You're born with a limited supply, you know. What if you sell them all, and you don't have any left for yourself?"

"Yeah, well, you know my luck with men."

"That could change—you're only thirty. Ben and I didn't get

together until I was thirty-two. It took me three years to get pregnant with Zoe, and we haven't used any birth control since then. Last spring I had some tests done. I'd give anything to have another baby, but it's not going to happen. What I'm saying is the way you feel about having kids can change a lot."

"Nope. I'm not meant to have kids. I am a little worried about cancer though. Two of the places made me sign an agreement that said I can't sue them if I get ovarian cancer."

"Oh, Clare, stop. Stop now."

"Yeah, I should, but it's hard to stop. Fast money, and it gives me time to paint. I'm only bartending two nights a week now. Next month after they harvest me, I'm going to quit my job and go to Mexico to paint for six weeks."

"That's great," Melissa says, but her arms feel heavy. The last time Clare quit her job, she stayed with Melissa and Ben for three months. That was before Zoe was born, but even then it had been too much. Ben couldn't stand Clare's cigarette smoke, and Melissa couldn't stand the guys Clare brought home after the bars closed.

Clare touches her shoulder. "Come on. We'd better get to bed. The train leaves in a few hours."

In the queen-sized bed with its stained lime-green bedspread, Melissa regrets drinking the coffee. Her body aches, and her eyes burn, but her mind won't stop buzzing. She can tell that Clare's awake too, in spite of all the drinks she's had.

Melissa tries to forget what's bothering her most, but she can't, and finally she asks, "Did you tell them about Jamie?"

"Who?"

"The egg donation places."

"What about him? They asked how many siblings I have, and I said one."

"About his hospitalizations. His mental illness."

"Jamie wasn't crazy. It's sane to leave a place when things get too ugly."

"You didn't tell them, did you?"

"No."

"And about Aunt Sylvia carbon-monoxiding herself in the garage?"

"She was married to that sadist. He wore her down."

"And Uncle Andrew, getting shock treatments back in the fifties? Manic depression runs in families."

"Well, so does everything else."

"Still, you ought to tell them."

"Well, when it first came up, I thought about it. Then I thought about you and decided it must be worth the risk."

"What about me?"

"You knew about Jamie and Aunt Sylvia and Uncle Andrew, and you went ahead and had Zoe."

"That's different."

"Is it?"

The question hangs in the stale air of their nonsmoking room in the Lucky Lady Hotel.

Clare says, "Just because you're married and respectable doesn't mean your eggs are any saner than mine."

"The difference is," Melissa says, "I chose to take the risk, but you're not giving those other people a choice."

"They never get the whole story. Do you think anybody who's trying to sell her eggs tells the complete truth about her family? Besides, so what if somebody has a baby like Jamie? They should be so lucky!"

As she drifts toward sleep, Melissa sees Clare turning into

the thirteenth fairy at the christening, the one who puts a curse on the baby in *Sleeping Beauty*. Melissa scrambles to find a charm for Zoe to ward off madness. She summons Zoe's dimples, her laugh, how early she slept through the night, but of course Jamie had been just like that, right down to the dimples.

At seven Clare wakes Melissa, and they stumble into a taxi that takes them to the station. Clare's out of money, so Melissa pays the taxi driver. Almost everyone on the fun train is dozing as it winds back through the Sierras toward San Francisco, but Clare is wide awake and fidgeting in her seat. As soon as Melissa sits down next to her in the observation car with her Styrofoam cup of coffee, Clare leans toward her.

"After we talked last night, I couldn't get to sleep, so I got dressed and went down to the casino to play draw poker on the nickel machines. Just as the sun came up, I got a royal flush! The lights flashed, and the bells rang, and it came to me. We can do it! You and I and Ben."

Melissa braces herself to tell her no, they can't all live together when Clare gets back from Mexico, but Clare says, "*We* can have the Jamie baby!"

A lake so blue it looks unreal comes into view. Melissa stares at it and tries to fathom what Clare is offering.

"I'll give you the eggs. Use Ben's sperm. You have the baby. You and Ben raise it."

"And what do you do?"

"I paint, and I get to watch him grow up."

"Clare, it wouldn't be Jamie," Melissa says, but Clare just shrugs and smiles like she has inside information.

The train rocks them through the evergreens, and Melissa

closes her eyes and imagines saying yes. She hears the women at work squeal when she tells them she's pregnant. In her mind's eye, she becomes large, calm, and powerful like she was when Zoe was growing inside her. She sees a photo of Zoe, jealous and proud, holding the new baby on the flowered sofa. She sees more photos: two children holding up their baskets at Easter, splashing in a wading pool in July, opening presents beside a Christmas tree.

In the Christmas picture, the younger child becomes Jamie. Now he's five, playing in the snow on the hill behind Gran and Gramps' barn. "Come on!" says Melissa, who's ten, but Jamie grins at her and scrambles onto a rusty old hay wagon. He wipes the snow off the seat with his mittens, climbs on it, stands up, and bounces up and down to make the springs squeak. "No!" Melissa yells, but Jamie just jumps higher. His feet fly out from under him, and he falls backward. Melissa hears him scream and runs toward him, her boots slipping in the wet snow. When she reaches him, his arms and legs are thrashing wildly, and for one giddy moment she thinks he's making a snow angel. His movements are jerky and scary, though, and a red stain is spreading on the snow. Melissa kneels to pull him toward her. One prong of a pitchfork has pierced his shoulder and is poking through the front of his snowsuit. She crawls around behind him, puts a foot on his back, and pulls the pitchfork out. She carries him down to the house, both of them screaming until their father opens the back door. Their mother, who's pregnant with Clare, gets hysterical and shakes Melissa again and again, demanding, "How could you let this happen?" After the ambulance comes, Gran rocks Melissa to sleep.

Memories of Jamie's other close calls, thirty years' worth of them, rise up in Melissa. She remembers how she and her dad tried to save him, over and over, her mother screaming accusations from the sidelines. She wonders why Clare worshipped his every move, right up to and including the day last February when he skied with consummate skill around a barricade and straight over a two-hundred-foot drop.

I can't, Melissa decides and turns to Clare. In the harsh morning light, Clare's face is so haggard and radiant that Melissa can't tell her. All she can do is hold her sister's hand and cry.

Split Shift

You can't waste a single move during the lunch rush at the Harvey House Restaurant in Lamy, New Mexico—a hundred passengers have forty minutes to eat before the whistle calls them back onto the train. Add the twenty guests of El Ortiz Hotel next door, and there's not even room for everybody to sit down at once. Waitresses don't have time to catch their breath, let alone chat, so I couldn't believe it when Leo hissed, "Bertie, come here!" and nodded toward the back of the kitchen. I set three plates of chicken croquettes back on the counter and followed him to the corner behind the ovens. There was Lorraine, her face as pale as her starched apron.

"Get someone to take over for me, Bertie," she said. "I can't go out there."

"We're short as it is," I told her, "and the place is full."

"I'm sorry, Bertie. I just can't." She started crying. I would have put my arms around her if Leo hadn't been there, but since he was, I just patted her arm.

"Don't cry, Lorraine. I'll take care of it," I said, even though it was going to make things impossible for everybody.

I served my table and then ran over to the lunch counter and told Jeanne I needed her to take over Lorraine's section. She said, "I can't do my own and hers—they're standing three deep!"

"Just do it," I told her. "I'll help you when I can."

Back in the dining room, meals weren't moving out yet. Every table was full, and the girls were still going around taking orders. I dashed into the kitchen and took the first ticket off the line.

"What happened to Lorraine?" I asked Leo as I snatched up a veal loaf special and a side of mashed potatoes.

"There's someone out there she doesn't want to see," he said.

The rest was just a blur of moving the late orders out to the lunch counter and then catching up my own section in the dining room. While we were serving dessert, Jeanne came into the dining room and said, "A man at the counter's asking for Lorraine."

"Let me talk to him," I told her, and we headed toward the lunchroom, but just then the train whistle blew, signaling the five-minute warning. There was a stampede toward the door, and we were pushed back into the dining room.

Even without seeing the man, I had the feeling a bad wind was starting up, the kind that used to carry off the crops on our farm back home. When the last customers had scrambled out of the dining room, stuffing rolls in their pockets and wiping their mouths on the backs of their hands, Jeanne and I went into the lunchroom. I let myself hope that the man had gone too, but one customer was still sitting at the counter. I stood and watched his broad back for a moment before Jeanne said in a loud whisper, "That's him."

He turned around slowly, and I have never before or since seen such a hard face. His weathered skin was scored with deep frown lines, and he squinted at us as if we'd just tried to cheat him. "Where's Lorraine?" he asked.

"In her room," I told him.

He wiped his lips, threw down his napkin, and stood up. I could see the gray hairs bristling in his nostrils and smell the mildew and stale sweat that clung to his black wool suit. "Take me to her," he said.

"I can't. Men aren't allowed in the women's dormitory."

"Then tell her to come here."

"She can't," I said. "She's sick." I'm sure I blushed from my lie.

"Who's in charge here?" he asked.

"The manager," I told him, "but he's gone to Topeka to meet with Mr. Fred Harvey." This at least was true, thank God.

"Then who's in charge in his absence?" he asked through tight lips. He took a step toward me, and I stood up to my full height, which is considerable for a woman.

"Leo is. He's the chef," I told him. "Jeanne, send Leo out here."

Jeanne headed toward the kitchen. The man started to follow, but I blocked his way. Jeanne looked back, frightened for me, but I motioned for her to go ahead.

I am no stranger to the anger of men. When I told my father I'd gotten a job as a Harvey Girl, he took off his belt and said, "No daughter of mine is going to work as a whore." I told him the girls live in dormitories with housemothers and have curfews, but it didn't make any difference to him. "You're not going," he said.

"I am going," I told him. "Go ahead and beat me—it's the last chance you'll ever have."

My back was covered with welts the next day when I took the train from Hutchinson to Topeka to get my training. I had to be careful to undress in the dark so the other girls wouldn't see what kind of family I had come from.

Training was tough, but we started right off at full salary, $17.50 a month. Since room and board were free, lots of the girls sent their wages home. I didn't ever do that. I started saving to buy myself a farm back in Kansas, not too near my family but near enough that my brother could come and visit. I often imagined him reporting to my father how successful my farm had become and how that would gall him.

"The kitchen is off-limits," I told the man in the Harvey House lunchroom. "You have to wait here."

He looked at me with such a fury that I could almost feel his hands closing on my neck, but I held my ground and put on the blank look that sometimes used to save me from beatings back home. The muscles in his jaw clenched, and he breathed heavily through his nose. He sounded just like a bull. I thought for a moment he was going to lower his head and charge into the kitchen, but the moment passed, and he sat back down at the counter. I automatically picked up the coffee pot and refilled his cup.

When Leo came in, the man stood up and towered over him. "I'm Anton Chambers, and I have come for Lorraine," he told him.

"I'm very surprised you say it," Leo said. "Lorraine told me her father is died."

Leo doesn't always use English the regular way, since he is from Germany. He was a famous chef there and even cooked for the Kaiser, as he often reminds us.

Anton Chambers snorted. "I'm not her father, you fool—I'm her husband."

Leo looked at me with raised eyebrows. Of course we both thought Anton was lying. The man looked sixty, and Lorraine's only twenty. Besides, Fred Harvey doesn't hire married women to work in his restaurants, and Lorraine had been a waitress there for a year and a half.

"I'm taking her home," he told us. "Are you going to go tell her to get packed, or do I have to go get her myself?"

Leo's very bossy in the kitchen, but he's a small, civilized man, no match for Anton Chambers. He scratched the bald spot in the middle of his thin orange hair and said, "You must to talk to the manager."

Anton snorted. "You think I'm going to wait around for him to get back from Topeka? I'm leaving on the six o'clock train tonight, and Lorraine is coming with me."

Clive, our dishwasher, came through carrying a big wooden crate the train had left off. He asked Leo where he wanted it. Ordinarily, Leo would get mad at Clive for interrupting him, but this time he smiled and motioned for him to come over. I think he wanted Anton Chambers to get a good look at Clive, who is at least a head taller than Anton and has a wild look about him that makes people stay out of his way.

Leo untwisted the wires on the crate and opened the refrigerated carton inside. He pulled out a slab of meat. "Rack of lamb," he said. "Tonight's special." He smelled it, nodded, and put it back in the carton. He wiped his bloody hands on his apron and said, "We have to work now." He looked at Anton and then at the door.

Anton folded his big arms and stood there glaring at us. I went over to the lunch counter and started clearing plates. He just stood there, so I told him, "You can wait in the lobby of the hotel, right through there."

He still didn't budge until Clive made a grunting sound down in his throat and cracked his knuckles. Then Anton told me, "You bring her down here!" and stomped out.

As soon as the door closed behind him, Leo pointed a blood-stained finger at the door and said, "No good."

"What does he want?" Clive asked.

"He wants to take Lorraine away," I told him.

Clive's lip curled, and his head jerked like it does when he gets upset. Once when Leo was screaming at him to hurry up and get the silverware washed, Clive's head started jerking like that, and he pulled a butcher knife out of the drawer and went after Leo. If Lorraine hadn't been there to talk him down, he would have cut him, maybe killed him. The manager fired Clive, but there was nobody else to do the job, and the dishes started to stack up, so he had to hire him back the next day.

I went into the dining room to check that the girls were cleaning the coffee urns, polishing the pastry cases, and folding the heavy linen napkins for dinner, and then I went to the dormitory to look for Lorraine. She wasn't there. For a horrible moment I thought that Anton had found her and dragged her off somewhere, so I rushed back to the hotel lobby. He was sitting there alone with his feet propped up on his valise. Most people who pass through Lamy fall in love with El Ortiz Hotel, but Anton obviously wasn't enchanted by the traditional log-beam ceilings or the rich colors of the Navajo rugs. He sat scowling at the empty fireplace and drumming his fingers on the arm of his chair.

I left without him seeing me and slipped down the path behind the hotel. It led through a patch of scrub brush and then up to a rocky ridge where Lorraine and I used to take some fresh air between shifts.

It was up there that we had our first fight. Lorraine had been in Lamy for three months, and we'd become friends. On that particular day, though, she was silent while we walked up the path on our break. When we got to the top, she proceeded to tell me that I was too hard on the girls. She said her roommate had cried herself to sleep the night before because of harsh words I'd said to her when she spilled a tray of fruit cocktails.

Of course I didn't like hearing it. I told Lorraine she'd better not criticize me until she'd been head waitress herself. Instead of saying something mean back to me, she took my hand and said everyone respected me and all I needed to do was be patient with the girls because they were scared and homesick.

When it was time to go back down, Lorraine asked if I was angry with her. I said I was, but I was also glad she'd had the gumption to tell me the truth, and I still wanted to be her friend. She was so relieved that she threw her arms around me and kissed my cheek. I just melted, and before I knew it, my arms were around her, and then we kissed for a long time. It was the only time I've ever been late to work.

That night she came to my room and stayed. She came again the next night, and the next day I told the manager Lorraine and her roommate weren't a good match, so Lorraine was moving in with me. It was fine with him, and that's just how it was from then on.

On Valentine's Day, I gave Lorraine the Irish ring my grandmother gave me when I was sixteen. The ring is made up of two hands holding a heart with a crown on it. Since it's against Harvey rules to wear jewelry, Lorraine wore it on a chain around her neck, under her uniform, and only we two knew it was there and what it meant.

I'd always gone to the ridge with Lorraine. As I hurried along by myself after leaving Anton Chambers at the hotel, the place felt unfriendly, even dangerous. Finally I spotted Lorraine on a flat rock in the shadow of a twisted pine. She was lying so still that it made my heart jump in my chest. I picked up my skirt and ran to her, stumbling over rocks and fallen branches. When I got near, she turned her face toward me, and for a moment I doubted that she was Lorraine. Her chestnut hair was disheveled, and her face was smudged with dirt.

"I won't go back, Bertie," she said, her voice as hollow as a ghost's.

"Of course you won't," I said and sat down on the rock beside her and held her in my arms. Ravens swooped down and perched in the tree above us. For a long time their hoarse cries and her sobbing were all you could hear.

Finally I had to ask her. "Why did he say you're his wife?"

"Because I am," she said.

I thought I knew everything about Lorraine, everything she'd done and everything she wanted to do. Now she seemed like a stranger, and I pulled away from her.

"When I was fifteen," she said, "my mother had a nervous disease that kept her bedridden, and my father's consumption got so bad that he couldn't keep teaching violin lessons. We were starving. Anton's sister lived next door, and one day she came over with a letter from him. He'd told her to find him a strong, young woman to marry because his wife had died and he had three children to raise. He promised to help my family, so my parents sent me off to Illinois to marry him."

"Why didn't you tell me?" I asked.

"At first I didn't tell you because I was afraid of losing my job. Later I just didn't want you to know about him."

"It wasn't your fault," I said. "You could have told me."

"No, Bertie," she said, looking down. "I couldn't bear to tell you. Anton was fifty when we got married. Two of his sons were older than I was, and they were rough like Anton. The three of them treated me in ways that are unspeakable." She looked up at me, and her face looked much older than twenty.

"Anton's youngest son was delicate and sweet, the only

goodness in my life there, but when he got ill, Anton wouldn't pay for a doctor, and I had to watch him die. The day after he was buried, I ran away to my cousin in Chicago, and she helped me get a job with Fred Harvey."

"Why has Anton come all this way to get you now?" I asked her.

Lorraine looked out over the dry hills. "He thinks I'm his," she said. "He gave my father one hundred and fifty dollars a year for the three years I was with him."

"But surely he got his money's worth from all the work you did," I said. I wouldn't let myself think about what else he demanded of her.

"Anton wouldn't see it that way," Lorraine said. "He has his own rules. Back in Illinois he got angry at a hired hand who missed a few days of work during the harvest. The man was sick, but Anton said it was all in his head, and he refused to pay him for any of the work he'd already done. The hired hand disappeared in the night on one of Anton's horses. Anton didn't discover the horse was missing for two days, but when he found out, he got on his fastest horse and went after him, leaving the harvest half finished. He followed the man for a week and finally caught up with him. He said that he gave him the beating he deserved, but I suspect he killed him.

"As Anton was returning home, bad weather blew in. He remembered all the wheat lying in the fields, and he drove the horses so hard that the older one dropped. He stopped only long enough to butcher the horse and load the meat onto the back of the horse he was riding. He whipped his horse all the way home, but he didn't make it in time. The rains had come, and they destroyed every last stalk of wheat. 'Let it rot,' he yelled as he rode into the yard on his bloody horse. 'I have got back what is mine.'"

I felt sick. "Clive can kill him for you," I said.

"No, Bertie. Then I'd have God after me instead of Anton," she said.

"God would understand."

"No," Lorraine said.

I looked down the ridge and realized for the first time how small the train station and the restaurant and hotel really were, just tiny specks in the wilderness. All around us was open country, as far as the eye could see. There were no friendly neighbors who would take us in.

If Lorraine wouldn't let Clive get rid of Anton, what were we going to do? Anton wouldn't leave without her, but I couldn't let her go. I couldn't imagine myself without Lorraine—sleepy Lorraine squeezing oranges with me as the sun rose, Lorraine riding beside me in the high country on Sundays, Lorraine making me laugh with her imitations of Leo, Lorraine rubbing my sore feet with almond oil at the end of a long day.

I asked Lorraine if she and Anton had gotten married in front of a judge. She said he'd refused to waste the money for that—he just wrote their names in the family Bible and said that was record enough. I told her we should hire a lawyer to cancel the marriage. Surely there was protection for a girl whose parents had made her marry an old man! I began to feel hopeful as I laid it out, but Lorraine said even if we could get a lawyer to give us a piece of paper, it wouldn't stop Anton. He had enough money to hire a better lawyer, and he would never give up until he beat us.

Lorraine and I lay there on the rock, lost, until the shadows crept east and a chill came into the air. The ravens rose together into the bright sky, scolding us as they left. I knew then it was up to me, and it is not in my nature to take things lying down.

"Let's go back," I said. I figured the restaurant would be the safest place for Lorraine for the time being because Clive would keep Anton away from her. As we walked down the path, I kept my arm around Lorraine's waist while my mind raced ahead to the powder I had in my top drawer.

I'd gotten it during my first months of working in New Mexico, when I couldn't get used to the dry air and the coyotes howling at night. I had dark circles under my eyes almost all the time, so the manager got me some sleeping medicine in Kansas City. Of course, after Lorraine came, everything changed, and I didn't have to use the powder anymore unless I drank coffee late in the day.

Back in our room at the dormitory, while Lorraine washed her face and put up her hair, I tucked a packet of the powder into my apron pocket. Together we went down the back way to the kitchen. Lorraine was a bundle of nerves, so I got Leo to make her a chicken salad sandwich, and I brought her a cup of tea.

I took an empty coffee pot to the urn in the dining room, but right away the girls came over to ask after Lorraine. I told them she'd be back on the job for dinner. They stayed there chatting on and on until I finally had to go to the coffee urn in the lunchroom.

I filled the pot a third full and then dumped in all the powder—five doses. I stirred the powder into the coffee and then poured some into a cup and tried it. It tasted a little bitter, but not awful. I worried that the coffee would work against the effects of the sleeping powder, but I couldn't think of any other way to give it to him without making him suspicious, so I took the coffee pot and a cup and saucer over to the hotel lobby.

Anton was pacing in front of the fireplace.

"Coffee?" I asked him.

"Where's Lorraine?" he asked. "It's 4:30."

"She's sleeping," I said. "Would you like some coffee?"

He grabbed my arm. "You get her now. I'm not waiting any longer."

"All right," I said, jerking my arm away from him. My hands were shaking, but I poured the coffee and handed it to him.

My arm hurt where he'd grabbed me, and I wanted nothing more than to get away from the sight and smell of him, but I couldn't leave without seeing if he would drink the coffee. "Would you like something to eat?" I asked. "Some applesauce cake or peach cobbler? Or maybe some lemon cream pie?"

Oh, my! The transformation that came over him! His mouth went from a straight, tight line to a moist circle. His eyes widened, and they were a warm brown, almost gold. He licked his lips, and I saw that somewhere, a long time ago, someone had loved him and had baked sweet things for him to eat.

"Peach cobbler," he said after long deliberation.

He took a drink of coffee, and I went to the kitchen. I took him a big bowl of peach cobbler with a little pitcher of fresh cream to put on it. He reached for his wallet, but I said, "No, this is on the house," and I smiled and refilled his coffee cup the way I'd been taught in Harvey Girl training.

Then I went back into the dining room and helped the girls set up for the dinner rush. After about twenty minutes, I took Anton a square of applesauce cake. He blinked at me, confused, and passed me his cobbler bowl, which looked like it had been licked clean. When I handed him the cake, he nodded and almost smiled. I poured him another cup of coffee, the last one in the pot, and went back to work.

Half an hour later, I took Anton a wedge of lemon cream pie, but he was in no condition to eat it. He was slumped down in the big leather chair with his legs stretched out in front of him. The empty cake plate was on the floor next to him. For a moment he looked so quiet that I was afraid I'd overdone the dosage, but then he let out a huge, rattling snore. A young couple across the lobby smiled at me, as people do when somebody snores in public. I cleared away his coffee cup and the cake dish and hurried to the kitchen.

Leo was in a frenzy, basting rolled racks of lamb with mustard paste and sprinkling them with seasoned bread crumbs. The kitchen smelled of garlic and mustard and sizzling lamb. The tart smell of apple pies baking came from the back ovens. This was my favorite meal, and I hadn't eaten anything since lunch. Lorraine was there having another cup of tea, and for a moment I weakened and thought about sitting down next to her, eating dinner, and leaving the rest up to God the way she always said we should, but I just couldn't. I motioned for Leo to come out to the dining room with me.

"Anton Chambers is asleep in the hotel lobby," I told him, "and I need you and Clive to put him on the train when it comes."

"Are you crazy?" Leo said.

"No," I told him. "He won't wake up. I gave him some powder."

"You killed him!"

"No, it was just sleeping powder."

"He's too big to carry."

"Clive can do it. You can just carry his feet."

"No. He might wake up. Besides, what are you going to tell the train people? I think we better to wait. This is for the manager to do."

"Please, Leo. Do it for Lorraine."

Leo shook his head and went back into the kitchen. I couldn't believe it. The little coward! When I went into the kitchen after him, he handed me a plate with the dinner special:

a thick slice of lamb, a scoop of Duchess potatoes and some string beans with almonds. I sat down by Lorraine and tried to eat, but I was too worried about Anton. I decided to go ahead without Leo.

I waited until Leo wasn't looking and then pulled Clive out the back door. I ignored his fierce look and told him, "We have to put that bad man on the train so he won't take Lorraine away." He made some growling sounds. I wasn't sure if he was mad at me or at Anton, but I took hold of his arm and led him over to the hotel. As we went into the lobby, I heard the train whistle, the signal that it would be arriving within minutes.

I was thinking ahead, planning to tell the conductor that Anton was drunk and to just let him sleep it off on the train. Then Clive and I rounded the corner. The chair where Anton had been sleeping was empty!

I asked the young couple in the lobby where he'd gone. They pointed to the door that led to the men's restroom out back.

"I'm sorry," I told Clive. "He was asleep right there a minute ago."

Clive kicked the chair and went back to the kitchen. I stood there staring at the chair. I couldn't believe Anton had woken up. Then I heard the mob from the train pouring into the restaurant, and all I could do was rush back to the dining room and start taking orders.

Anton didn't show up right away, and I wondered if maybe he'd gone to sleep in the men's room. Then just as we were serving the last meals, he stumbled into the restaurant. His eyes were red-rimmed, and his hair stood up in gray tufts.

He stood in the doorway until he spotted Lorraine, and then he sat down with an elderly couple at a table in her station. When Lorraine walked by with a coffee pot, he grabbed her wrist and pulled her close enough to whisper in her ear. As the color drained from her face, I felt my own heart pounding like a gong. In my mind's eye, I saw Anton riding home with the slaughtered horse behind his saddle, and it came to me, He won't leave empty-handed.

I went out the back door and up to my room. I unlocked my trunk, pulled out the tin box with my initials engraved on the lid, and sat down on the bed. I counted the money, even though I knew by heart how much there was. I put the change and seven one-dollar bills back in the box and put all the rest into my pocket.

When I got back to the dining room, Anton was alone at the table with the dinner special in front of him. He was chewing fast, glaring at Lorraine as she refilled coffee cups at the table where the train crew was sitting.

I sat down next to Anton. He turned toward me, and he looked like he was going to kill someone or start crying, I couldn't tell which.

"She's not going to leave," I told him.

"She has to," he said, his lips shiny with grease.

"No, she belongs here."

"I'll make her come. She's my wife."

"You can't. Those men run the train, and they're Lorraine's friends."

"Then I'll get the law, and I'll come back."

I could see by the set of his jaw that he meant it. He went back to mopping up gravy with bread and shoving it into his mouth, and we both watched Lorraine. The brakemen were joking with her, and although she was still pale, she laughed out loud.

"Ha!" Anton said, as if he'd caught her in the act. Of course I knew that it wasn't what he thought, but for a moment, I saw Lorraine through his eyes, and terrible doubts rose up in me. If she hadn't told me about Anton, what else had she kept from me? Maybe she did have special feelings for the fellow who had made her laugh. I felt separate from her, and I could hear my father's voice inside me saying, "She's made a fool of you!"

Then Lorraine looked over and saw me sitting with Anton. Her smile dropped away, and she gave me a private look, full of concern. She touched her heart, where my ring was hidden under her black shirtwaist and white apron, and her lips shaped my name.

Ha yourself, Anton! I thought. Lorraine is my girl, and the only fool here is the one sitting next to me.

I took a deep breath, reached into my apron pocket, and pulled out all the wages and tips I'd saved since I started working as a Harvey Girl.

"Here," I said to Anton. "Here's your money back"

"What money?" he said.

"The money you gave Lorraine's parents. You can have it back if you promise to let her go." I set the stack of bills on the table in front of me.

"Where did she get that kind of money?"

"Where do you think?" I asked him.

His eyes narrowed, and he looked from the money to Lorraine with a sneer on his face.

The train crew stood up and started toward the door. Passengers got up and followed after them. "The train's about to leave," I said.

Anton stared at the money and chewed his lip. Then he nodded.

I handed him my pad and pen and had him write on the back of one of the tickets, "Received, $450. May 29, 1914. Marriage with Lorraine is ended."

I made him go back in the kitchen and sign it in front of Leo, and I had Leo sign as a witness. Then I handed Anton the money. The warning whistle from the train sounded, but Anton stood there and counted the money twice before he put it into his worn leather wallet.

I followed him out to the platform and watched him get on the train. He sat down next to an open window. Lorraine ran up beside me and took my arm. "Oh, Bertie, he's leaving!" she said.

"Yes," I said.

Anton beckoned for us to come over. Lorraine pulled back into the shadows, but I went over to him.

"You can have her," he said. "Good riddance!"

I gave him my blankest look.

The train pulled out, and I watched it until it rounded the bend, taking Anton and my money east along the rails that brought me here. In the morning, Anton and my money would pass by my hometown and the people I missed and the people who had made me glad to leave home.

I looked west along the tracks that led to the places I'd never been: Albuquerque and Gallup and Flagstaff and Seligman and Kingman and Needles and Barstow and Los Angeles, and for the first time, their names sounded beautiful. For the first time I felt Lorraine was lucky to be loved by me, and for the first time I felt I belonged in the world and the world belonged to me whether I could buy it or not.

Meat

Serving a spinach soufflé was Raymond's first mistake. His father wouldn't even try it, and his mother picked at hers. When Raymond looked pained, his mother said, "Sorry, Ray, guess we're still meat and potatoes folks." His father asked for lunchmeat and made himself a sandwich with the Black Forest ham Raymond brought him, but after one bite he put down the sandwich and asked what the hell was wrong with the bread.

"It's supposed to be sour, Dad. It's a San Francisco tradition."

"Well, what else have you got?"

"Nothing," Raymond said and wished trap doors would open under his parents and drop them into plastic tubes that would suck them back to their potato farm in Idaho.

"If you don't eat your dinner, you won't get any dessert!" Raymond said.

"Ha, ha," his mother said nervously.

"That's what you used to tell me," Raymond said.

"Did we?" she asked, peeling a mint leaf off one of her carrots.

Raymond had no idea where to go from there, but his father

was prepared. "Seems like we saw a steakhouse on the way here, didn't we? Sort of out by the airport? Let's go."

Later, after the steakhouse and after his parents had gone to bed, Raymond fixed himself a plate of cold spinach soufflé and carrots and called Gina.

"Did you pave the way?" she asked.

"Not even close," Raymond said.

"Not to worry," Gina said. "We'll tell them together tomorrow night."

Raymond worried. He bought Idaho potatoes and ground round on the way home from work. His parents were watching the news on TV when he arrived. "My friend Gina is joining us for dinner," he called to them from the kitchen.

His mother came right in and sat on a stool next to him as he ground Parmesan cheese for the Caesar salad dressing. "A new friend?" she asked.

"No, I've known her for a couple of years. She teaches at City College too."

"Oh, that's nice. You must have a lot in common."

"Well, actually, we do, but Mom, I'm still with Martin. Gina's a friend-friend, not a girlfriend."

"Well, I wouldn't close any doors," his mother said brightly, cocking her head to one side.

Gina arrived, and to Raymond's relief she wasn't wearing her studded leather jacket. Raymond's parents were cordial, Gina was pleasant, the meatloaf looked perfect, and Raymond felt a rosy glow as he sat down at the head of the table.

"You put onions in this?" his father asked with his mouth full of meatloaf.

"Oh, dear, George can't eat onions," Raymond's mother said. "They don't agree with him."

"I like them, but they don't like me," Raymond's father said, pushing his plate away. He leaned back and folded his arms.

Gina watched the flush rising up Raymond's neck. "Barney's!" she said. "The best burgers in San Francisco, and it's only two blocks away. Let's go."

After Raymond's dad had eaten a charbroiled half pounder with cheddar and Raymond's mother had eaten a quarter pounder with cheddar and Gina had eaten a vegiburger with sautéed mushrooms and Raymond had eaten a Thai chicken salad, Gina caught Raymond's eye and whispered, "Now!"

"Mom, Dad, uh, Gina and I have something to tell you. She's going to have a baby, and, well, I'm the father."

Raymond's parents looked from Raymond to Gina, then at each other, then back at Raymond.

"So when's the wedding?" Raymond's mother asked cautiously.

"Oh, we're not going to get married. I have a partner," said Gina.

"Oh, dear," said Raymond's mother.

"No, it's fine. Marie loves Raymond too."

"I'm afraid I don't understand," said Raymond's mother.

"Would anybody care for dessert?" the waiter asked, and in unison Raymond and his father said, "Yes!" Over brownie sundaes for the parents and cappuccino cheesecake for Raymond and Gina, the four of them exchanged uneasy glances. Finally, Raymond's mother asked, "When is the baby due?"

Gina grinned. "August. August tenth is what they said."

Raymond's father put down his fork and said, "That's my birthday."

"Wow," Gina said. "What if it actually comes on that day?"

After they walked home, Gina drove away, and Raymond and his parents went inside. His father cleared his throat and asked, "Is she sure it's your baby? I mean if she's got another partner and still got together with you, how can you be sure there aren't others?"

Raymond laughed. "She's not sleeping around. We didn't have sex."

"Well, then how did she get pregnant?"

"Artificial insemination. I just gave her some sperm."

Raymond's father snorted and shook his head. "This is too much for me. I'm going to bed," he said, and he did. Reluctantly Raymond's mom followed him, and Raymond went to his own room.

While he changed into his pajamas, he wondered what his parents were saying about him and Gina and the baby. He wished he hadn't let Gina talk him into telling them face to face. His father's disgust made him queasy and threatened to bring up unbearable memories. To ward them off, he imagined his parents as Mr. And Mrs. Potato Head, putting on blue plastic hats and scurrying back to where they belonged on tiny red plastic feet. They got smaller and smaller, and when they disappeared, he went to sleep.

The next day after work he didn't stop to buy food. It was no use. He'd just take them to Barney's or the steakhouse, and the next morning they'd be gone. He couldn't wait.

When he got home, though, the house was empty, and he couldn't imagine where they might have gone. Then he heard voices in the backyard and smelled meat cooking. He opened the back door and saw his dad turning steaks on the barbeque and his mom slicing tomatoes on a TV tray. "Surprise!" she said. "We cooked dinner for you."

"You still like yours medium rare?" his father asked, and Raymond nodded.

A chilly wind came up, so they took the food inside. During the meal, they talked about things back home, the crops, the new shed, the people who had left and the people who had stayed on. For dessert his mother brought out homemade shortcake, fresh strawberries, and heavy whipped cream.

Nothing was said about the baby, but the next day at the airport, right before they boarded the plane, his mother said, "In August, if you need me, I'll come." She blushed, and she and Raymond's father disappeared into the airplane.

Chosen

Marilyn knows she shouldn't look at herself when she feels like this, but of course she goes straight to the bathroom and turns on the light over the mirror. Immediately she regrets it. How could she have aged so many years in one day? She looked good after her workout this morning, flushed and bright-eyed. And before her audition, with all her makeup on, she'd thought, "Not bad!"

It was the audition. Not getting the part has made her ugly. Or maybe being ugly made her not get the part. Or maybe it was being old. Or maybe her being old *and* ugly made them not choose her.

Marilyn remembers her grandmother. Just before they put her into a nursing home, she'd gone through her family albums and cut herself out of all the pictures taken after she turned fifty. Marilyn and her mother had thought it a crazy thing to do at the time—more evidence that Grammy shouldn't be living alone.

Marilyn's fifty. She's used to the wrinkles at the outer edges of her eyes, but tonight she notices a crinkly texture on the skin above the bridge of her nose, between her eyes. She puts on a pair of reading glasses, gets up close to the mirror and sees with horror that a new wrinkle zone has appeared. She begins to understand why a person would cut herself out of the picture.

As Marilyn stares into her bathroom mirror in San Francisco, her niece, Susie, studies her own reflection in the dark window of a Greyhound bus rolling north through California's Central Valley. Her son, Toby, is curled up under her jacket on the seat next to hers. He whimpers, and she pulls a bottle of apple juice out of the diaper bag and shoves the nipple into his mouth.

Susie gets a compact out of her purse, turns on her overhead light, and takes a closer look at her face. Her right eyelid is purple with some red and yellow around the edges, and her lip is still swollen, even though it's been five days since Wayne knocked her around.

She smoothes some foundation around her eye and powders over it. She applies lipstick to her mismatched lips. Then she digs around in her purse and pulls out the bus ticket that she got from the social worker at the battered women's shelter yesterday. One-way to Portland. She digs deeper and finds Larry Reynolds' card. She hopes he'll remember her when she shows up at Larry's Lair tomorrow. It's been over three months since he offered her the job. She and Larry had been dancing together while Wayne was off dealing or hitting on some woman, and Larry had said, "You really know how to move. Have you ever danced professionally?" She giggled, and that's when he said, "I'd give you a job in a minute! Come see me if you ever make it up to Portland."

Susie frowns as she puts everything back into her purse. She's only eighteen, but she's worried about her face. She's afraid it's going to keep her from getting a job.

In Salinas one passenger gets on. He lugs a khaki duffel bag up the aisle and sits down across from her. His haircut is Army-issue, or maybe Marine. As soon as he gets settled in the seat next to the window, he raises a flask to his lips. She watches him until he turns to look at her, and then she smiles, a big smile that pulls her lip against her teeth. It hurts, but it's worth it. He smiles back and nods for her to come and sit next to him, and she turns off her overhead light and joins him.

Marilyn turns off the bathroom light and pours herself a glass of white wine. She tries not to think about the audition, but certain moments keep coming back, especially the moment when she had to wait forever for a line to come to her.

She tries to imagine the neural pathways in her brain, to trace what's gone awry. She's always been a quick study, the first to learn her lines. Lately, though, something's amiss, and tonight the missing lines weren't just hesitating in the wings—they'd left the theater.

She turns away from the dark mirror. No use worrying about wrinkles. She decides she didn't get the part because she couldn't remember her lines. Of course that might have been because she wasn't wearing her lucky pendant, the one with the tiny lapis lizard on it. The guy who sold it to her in Santa Fe told her lapis enhances memory, and the lizard is the keeper of dreams. She never goes onstage without it—or she hadn't until tonight.

She couldn't find it before work this morning, so she searches for it now in her jewelry box, in her makeup case, in the bottom of her purse. These are exactly the same places she looked this morning, and that makes her think of the operational definition of insanity: Doing the same thing in the same way and expecting a different result. She gets a yardstick and swishes it back and forth under her dresser, but all that comes out is dust. She decides it's time to quit looking, not just for the lizard but for the dreams he was supposed to be keeping for her. She will apply herself to substantial things from now on, pursuits with a bottom line. How easy it will be! In her thirty years as an office temp, she's had hundreds of offers to go permanent. Just this morning, the Dean of Student Services at the private university where she's working practically begged her to accept a permanent position as his Administrative Aide. He mentioned health insurance, vacation pay, a retirement package. No interview—no audition. Just twenty years of playing Kathryn Hepburn to the Dean of Students' Spencer Tracy in *Desk Set*. A role to last a lifetime. Never another audition.

Of course, Marilyn admits, the dean is not at all like Spencer Tracy. He's dull and pompous, and the job is tedious. But that's all to the good. If even a fraction of her brain remains functional, she'll be able to maintain, and she'll never ever think of doing another play.

She starts taking photos of herself from the wall: herself as Nora in *A Doll's House*, herself as Blanche in *A Streetcar Named Desire*, herself as Amanda Wingfield in *The Glass Menagerie*. The pictures seem pathetic to her tonight. She played Nora in a college production and Blanche and Amanda in community theatre productions so small the critics didn't bother to review them. The rest of the time she's played neighbors and secretaries and aunts and maids and—lately—grandmothers. *Enough*, she decides. *Enough of throwing my heart into worlds that vanish into thin air.*

She whispers, "This rough magic I here abjure."

In the dark bus, the whiskey works its magic on Susie, and she turns to the soldier beside her and sees that he's much cuter than she'd thought at first. He offers her the last sip, but she insists that he finish it.

In San Jose the hunched, gray-faced bus driver gets off, and a new young one with a blond ponytail gets on. He announces their arrival times in San Francisco, Santa Rosa, and Eureka. As soon as the bus rolls out of the city and eases into darkness, the soldier unzips the duffel bag at his feet and pulls out another pint of whiskey. He opens it and hands it to Susie. "Ever been to San Francisco?" he asks.

Susie closes her eyes and sips the whiskey. She's been to San Francisco, but she doesn't like to remember it.

"It's a great city," he says and lets his hand rest on her thigh. "I've had some great times there. Some of the best times of my life."

Susie is having a great time right there on the bus. For the first time in five days, nothing hurts, and everything is easy again. When the soldier puts his arm around her and says, "Let's get off in San Francisco! I can show you around," she smiles up at him and says, "Why not?"

They glide through the night in an amber glow until the bus stops and it's time to get out.

"You have a kid?" the soldier asks when Susie gathers up Toby and the diaper bag and looks under their seats for Toby's stuffed giraffe. She doesn't answer, just carries Toby down the aisle. The soldier thinks maybe he's made a mistake and looks back at his seat, but Susie is waiting for him at the front of the bus, and he follows her down the aisle and out into the chilly night air. While she waits for someone to unload her suitcase, he goes into the men's room and finishes off the pint.

Marilyn finishes her glass of wine and puts the pictures on the top shelf of her closet. On the wall where Nora, Blanche, and Amanda hung, there are rectangles that are a paler white than the rest of the wall.

The pictures are only the beginning of what needs to go. She has to get rid of stacks of old scripts, boxes of scrapbooks, address books with out-of-date phone numbers for theater friends who never stop moving. "Gypsies," her last boyfriend used to call them. He was an accountant and didn't last long.

Marilyn dumps an armload of scripts into the recycling bin and lies down on the sofa. She stares at the white rectangles on the wall, and wave after wave of emptiness sweeps over her. It feels like nausea but comes from someplace deeper than the pit of her stomach.

Her doorbell rings. She looks at her watch and frowns. Ten thirty. "Who is it?" she asks over the intercom. "Susie," her niece replies, and Marilyn's frown gets deeper. She has to buzz her in, her sister Julia's daughter.

Marilyn opens the door and almost closes it when she sees Susie's bruised face and the surly face of the soldier beside her.

"Can I please use your restroom, ma'am?" the soldier asks as soon as she lets them in. She feels his eyes moving over her as she leads him down the hall.

When he comes out and sits on the sofa beside Susie and the still-sleeping Toby, Marilyn can't stop herself from rising to the occasion. "Would you like something to drink?" she asks them.

Both Susie and the soldier lean forward eagerly, and she adds, "Some mineral water or maybe coffee?"

"Coffee would be good," the soldier says, and Susie follows her aunt into the kitchen. The soldier crosses the room and sinks into a red velvet armchair, enchanted by the antique mauve lampshade and the magenta scarf draped over the table next to it. He grew up in a trailer outside of Phoenix where nothing had been chosen for its color or the way it would feel to the touch. He sees there's no bedroom and wonders where everyone will sleep tonight.

In the kitchen, Susie asks, "Could we stay with you for a couple of days, Aunt Marilyn? It would really help us out."

"No, Susie," Marilyn says, surprised how easy it is to tell her no.

The last time she saw Susie was when she'd brought her new baby to show to Julia a few weeks before she died of breast cancer. Toby had been fretful and jumpy because he was withdrawing from all the drugs and alcohol he'd been blasted with in utero, and Julia had been too weak to hold him. Marilyn had sat next to Julia on the bed and held the baby and tried not to hate Susie for asking her dying mother for $500. "For the baby," she'd assured them. "It's not for me."

Now Susie pouts. "Well, how about just for tonight?"

"It's a studio, Susie. There's no room."

"Well, can you at least take care of Toby while we go to the corner and get him some diapers? We're all out, and he's going to get a rash."

"All right."

"We'll come right back and change him and go get a motel."

While Marilyn sets cups and saucers on a tray, Susie goes to the bathroom to freshen up. After she brushes her hair and touches up her makeup, she automatically opens the medicine cabinet and scans the shelves. Between a bottle of Change-O'-Life herbs and a jar of extra-rich eye renewal cream she finds a full bottle of Vicodin. She takes one pill and slides the rest into the pocket of her leather jacket.

She checks the other shelves but finds nothing of interest except a tiny red satin purse with a gold snap. She opens it and pulls out a blue lizard on a gold chain. She remembers her aunt buying the necklace a long time ago on a trip to the Southwest with Susie and her mom. Back then Susie adored her aunt, and when Marilyn had told her the lizard was magic, she'd believed her. She starts to put the lizard back, but then she remembers that Marilyn is sending her away, so she takes it.

While Susie's in the bathroom, Marilyn brings the coffee into the living room. She'd like to get Susie and the soldier out the door before Susie has a chance to ask her for money for the diapers and the motel.

The soldier asks, "So, you work here in the City?"

"Yes, I . . . well, not really, not any more. Not my real work. Of course, I *work* here—we all have to work, don't we?"

The soldier nods and waits for Marilyn to ask him about himself, but she doesn't. She stares at the wall behind him as if he weren't there, so he pours milk into his coffee and drinks it fast. When Susie finally comes back, he jumps to his feet and steers her toward the door.

The service isn't great at City Nights, but the music is. Once Susie begins to dance, she inhabits only this moment in time. She's nobody's mother and nobody's daughter. She belongs to the music, and that's enough.

The soldier's a good dancer. It's something that comes easily to him, like playing pool, and he's good enough to appreciate what Susie's doing. In this light, moving in these ways, Susie makes him glad he interrupted his trip to see his buddy in Santa Rosa. When he pulls her in close for a slow dance, he can see how puffy her lip is, and it makes him want to kiss her hard.

At first it's not hard for Marilyn to come up with reasons for their absence. She thinks Susie and the soldier probably bought a bottle at the corner store, and they're sitting on someone's steps drinking it. After an hour, she thinks they probably stopped by the Tip-Top, right across from the store, and she resigns herself to a 2:00 a.m. return when the bar closes.

At 2:30 they're still not back, and Toby wakes up. He sits up on the sofa, looks around, and starts to cry. Marilyn picks him up, but he keeps crying. The longer it goes on, the more it seems to Marilyn he's crying not just for himself but for every unwanted person on the face of the earth.

Her upstairs neighbor pounds on his floor, but Marilyn doesn't know how to make Toby stop crying. All that comes to her mind is, *There's been a mistake. Julia should be holding this child, Julia, who had hundreds of dolls and started babysitting in fifth grade, Julia, who wanted children more than she wanted romance or a career, Julia, who would have loved being his grandmother.*

Marilyn puts a towel on the carpet and lays Toby on it. He cries harder as she tries to clean his bottom with a wet washcloth. She remembers Julia bathing Susie in the kitchen sink, and she carries Toby into the kitchen and runs a sink full of warm water and sets him in it. She washes him with dishwashing liquid and dries him and pins a clean dishtowel on him for a diaper.

He's still crying, so she gets some raspberry yogurt out of the refrigerator and feeds it to him. He gulps it down as fast as she can get it to his mouth. After he's eaten a second carton of yogurt, she digs around in the diaper bag Susie left and finds a yellow sleeper with feet and puts it on him.

Now she's sitting on the sofa with his warm weight on her lap. Something stirs in her, and she kisses his downy hair. He stares up at her with his dark eyes and then reaches up and pats her wrinkled cheek. His is the softest hand that has ever touched her.

In My Neighbor's Garden

I leaned over the fence and asked her straight out, "Have you bought that place?"

"Yes," she said and frowned at me like she was thinking, "Isn't it obvious?"

Well, it wasn't obvious. Married couples usually buy houses, and whatever she and that other one might be, they aren't a married couple. I don't care what they are, just so they turn down their music at 10:00 and keep the sidewalk clean in front of their house.

I decided not to beat around the bush. "You've got to get rid of that tree," I told her.

"Are you serious? The real estate agent told us it's the biggest redwood in Noe Valley. It's one of the reasons we chose the house."

"It drops things in my garden," I told her. "Horrible orange things that kill my plants."

She looked around her back yard, which was nothing but an overgrown thicket of weeds. "I don't see any orange things."

"You will. They start falling in September. You'll be up to your ankles in them."

She folded her arms. "We love this tree, and we're not going to cut it down."

I stared at her until she looked away, just to let her know I meant business. Then I turned around and went back inside.

That was the short, dark one I talked to. The other one is tall and has red hair. I had an uneasy feeling about them from the beginning, and my feeling turned out to be right. As soon as they settled in, they started putting out their garbage and recycling when they got home from work on Mondays, even through it isn't picked up until 6:15 on Tuesday morning. This means that recycling scavengers come by to dig through their bin at all hours of the night and make a racket looking for cans. Half the time, they dump everything out on the sidewalk so that all the papers blow over in front of my house.

One morning I made it a point to go down and sweep up their trash at 8:45, just as they were leaving for work. When they said, "Good morning," I said, "If you'd put out your recycling early in the morning, it wouldn't end up in front of my house every week."

The dark-haired one said, "Are you serious? They come at 6:00!"

"6:15," I told them, but I could see that didn't help. The red-haired one picked up a couple of TV dinner cartons and several pages of a newspaper that were in front of their garage door and put them into their recycling bin and carried it into the garage. The dark-haired one pulled the garbage cans in after her, and I called after them, "You could set an alarm!" I don't know if they heard me or not. All I know is they kept putting everything out on Monday afternoon.

Then after the rains stopped in April, they surprised me.

They started spending their weekends in their back yard, and they cleared out two years' worth of weeds and planted all kinds of flowers and vegetables. Of course, the insects and caterpillars got all of their vegetables except the zucchinis, but the flowers took hold, and it was nice to see the place turning into a garden again. The more work they put into it, the happier I got because I knew when autumn came, they'd find out what that tree was all about.

We had a hot September, and the orange things fell like rain. One Saturday, they were back there trying to rake them up without destroying their perennials. The red-haired one stopped working and rubbed her back. She turned profile toward me, and she was pregnant!

I doubted my eyes for a moment. These two weren't just roommates. I'd seen them kissing back there in the evenings. How in the world could one of them be pregnant?

I figured that maybe the red-haired one had gotten herself in trouble, and the dark-haired one had taken her under her wing, and they'd moved in together and then fallen in love. I counted up the months, though, and it didn't work out. They'd been kissing when they moved in back in January, nine months ago.

The red-haired one looked about six months pregnant. Had she been cheating on the other one, sneaking down to pick up men at that singles' bar on Twenty-Fourth Street? Or maybe she just slipped up one time, maybe with someone at work.

I didn't know whether to feel sorry for her or not. She's at least thirty-five—old enough to know better. Still, anybody can make a mistake. As I stood there watching from behind the camellia bush, I felt sorry for both of them.

That didn't last long. The next weekend, they had a big barbeque in their back yard with lots of homosexual couples, male and female, and a few regular couples with children. It happened to be one of the only warm evenings of the year in San Francisco, so I was out on my deck having a glass of ice tea and repotting some orchids.

The dark-haired one was talking with one of the married women right next to the fence.

"I hope you don't mind my asking," the married one said, "but how did you guys do it? Get her pregnant, I mean."

"Jonathon—over there—gave us some sperm."

"But . . . like . . . how? I mean, did they *do* it?"

The dark-haired one snorted. "No. Jonathon came over and went into the back bedroom and jerked off into a plastic cup. After he left, I inseminated her."

I was wearing my leather gardening gloves, and I didn't have a very good grip on my glass of ice tea. It slipped out of my grasp and smashed to pieces on the deck. The women by the fence stopped talking for a moment, but then the married one started up again.

"Did you use a turkey baster?"

"No, a small syringe."

"It seems kind of cold."

"Actually I warmed it up."

"No, I mean the whole—"

But she didn't get to finish because the dark-haired one had walked away.

I didn't have much contact with them for quite awhile after that. At Thanksgiving, I went back East to visit my sister. I told her about my neighbors, and she said lots of homosexual people in Boston are having babies, too. In fact, this woman engineer where her daughter works had a baby by using sperm she got from a sperm bank.

My sister always does that. No matter what I tell her, she can top it. She's done it to me my whole life, and it used to make me furious. After all these years, I thought I'd come to terms with it, but when she started going on about how the engineer looked through a big catalogue to choose her sperm donor, I found myself standing up for my neighbors. "At least," I told her, "they took the trouble to get it from someone they know!"

The morning after I got back from Boston, when I went down to get the paper, the red-haired one was sitting on my front steps crying.

"Are you all right?" I asked her.

"No," she said. "Look." She swung one of her feet onto the top step and pushed her finger into her ankle. It left a deep dent. "I'm puffed up like a sponge, and I have to pee every twenty minutes, and I never sleep. I've got carpal tunnel syndrome because of my edema, but I can't afford to stop working yet because I'm taking six weeks off after the baby comes."

"Maybe you could call in sick," I said.

"I used up all my sick leave when I was puking my guts out during the first trimester." She blew her nose. "I'm sorry. I'm sure you don't need to hear this so early in the morning." She hoisted herself up and went and got into her car. Her belly barely fit under the steering wheel.

"Take care," I said as she drove away, but I don't think she heard me.

After I read the paper, I went out back to work in the garden, but it started to rain. I came inside and brewed myself a cup of Sanka and worked on my knitting. I'd started an afghan on the plane coming home from my sister's.

I kept thinking about my neighbor having to work with those swollen ankles. I thought about how lucky I'd been, no morning sickness, just a big appetite and bouts of sleepiness. Then at six months, suddenly nothing, no movement, no heartbeat.

"It was just a fluke. Get pregnant again as soon as you can," the doctor told us, but Robert said absolutely not. He said I'd tricked him into the first one. He didn't even come to pick me up at the hospital after I delivered her. I had to take a taxi home.

The rain got heavier, and I kept knitting. The sound of the rain and the warmth from the heater made me so sleepy that I thought about making myself a cup of real coffee, but I knew I'd be sorry later. Instead I lay down on the sofa and covered myself with the afghan I knit last year. I was thinking about my neighbors and the baby and almost dozing off when I remembered something I hadn't thought about in years.

After I lost the baby, I sat in the nursery and rocked for days and days. I couldn't bring myself to put the baby things away. Robert worked late every night, and we barely saw each other. I didn't want to call anyone because I'd have to talk about what had happened. I knew I should call my sister, but I just couldn't.

Finally Robert told me I looked disgusting and I'd better get a grip on myself. I knew he was right, so I decided to get my hair done, but I didn't want to go to my regular hairdresser. I made an appointment with someone named Norma in a shop that had just opened down on Castro near Twenty-Fourth.

It was the strangest thing. As soon as Norma started washing my hair, I burst into tears and told her everything that had happened, all about the baby and even about Robert. I'd never laid eyes on her before, but I told her things I hadn't even told myself. I don't remember what she said to me. I think she mostly listened. Then while I was under the dryer, she left and came back with something in a white bakery bag. After she combed me out and I paid, she gave me the bag. Inside was a warm loaf of cinnamon raisin bread, unsliced.

When I got home, I didn't go into the nursery. I went into the kitchen and ate the bread. I didn't even slice it, just tore off handful after handful. After I'd eaten the whole loaf, I called my sister and told her what happened to me and the baby, and we cried together, and she jumped on a plane and came and helped me move out.

I got up and worked on my knitting. I clicked along for quite awhile with my mind drifting this way and that, and then I looked down at what I'd made. It looked more like a baby blanket than a half-finished afghan, so I cast it off my needles and finished the edges. Fortunately, I'd been using up some odds and ends of yarn—navy, maroon, gold, and white—that would be all right for either a girl or a boy. I wrapped it in tissue paper and put it on the table in the hall.

When I heard the neighbors' garage door opener rumble at 5:30, I checked out the front window to make sure it was the red-haired one, and I took the package downstairs. I waited until she came out of the garage, and I gave it to her. "For the baby," I said.

For a moment I was afraid she was going to hug me, but she stopped herself and patted my arm. "Thanks," she said and opened it right there on the sidewalk like people do here. "It's wonderful," she said and pressed it against her cheek. "Did you make it?"

"Yes," I said. "You'd better go in and put your feet up now."

"Thanks," she said, and we both went inside our houses.

After the baby's off to a good start, I'll bring up the tree again.

Zephyr

For solitary travelers, Christmas Eve is not an auspicious day to undertake a long journey by train. Doing so practically guarantees they'll spend the holiest of nights among strangers. Still, trains run on that day, and lost souls climb on board when they are too scattered to get home on time or have no home to get to.

Both of these things were true of Morgan. Perhaps that's why she appeared to lag even as she tried to rush. Perhaps that's why she was dragging her bags into the Emeryville station at 9:35 a.m. for a train that was scheduled to depart at 9:36 a.m.

"The *California Zephyr* is running ninety minutes late," the Amtrak agent told Morgan when she bellied up to the ticket counter.

"Well, that's not very zephyr-like!" Morgan said.

She had a cup of coffee, and then she went to the bathroom. Fifteen minutes later, she had to go to the bathroom again. The bathroom stalls were small, and Morgan and her suitcases were large, so before her second trip she asked an older woman with an honest-looking face to watch her bags.

The bags were large because Morgan was going to Denver for an extended stay. Morgan was large—and had to pee every few minutes—because she was pregnant.

Back in the waiting room, Morgan studied the other passengers. She noted that the woman who had watched her bags was the perfect choice if one needed a bag-watcher in a train station. She had white hair, rosy cheeks, a portly build, and upright posture. Her expression was pleasant but no-nonsense, and she was knitting a sweater out of red and green yarn. She could, Morgan reflected, be Mrs. Santa.

Other passengers were not so chipper and self-contained. "Get over here and sit the fuck down," a haggard woman barked at her three-year-old twin boys, who had identical red hair and unwiped runny noses. They ignored her and continued to chase each other across the feet of waiting passengers, tipping over suitcases as they ran.

A teenage girl in the seat next to Morgan whined on a cell phone, "It wasn't *my* idea. *I* never wanted to in the first place."

Morgan moved over next to the woman who had watched her bags. "Where are you headed?" she asked her.

"Well, I'm headed for Des Moines, but I'll be getting off in Osceola," the woman said. "How about you?"

"Denver," Morgan said.

"Going home for Christmas?" the woman asked.

"Yes, sort of," Morgan said.

"Hope you're ready for some cold weather. We're having quite a winter back there."

Morgan forced a thin smile and shrugged. In spite of all the sweaters in her suitcase, she knew she wasn't ready for cold weather or the baby or any of the other things that were inexorably coming her way. She hadn't been ready to be deserted on Thanksgiving, had been so pitifully unready, in fact, that she had come to feel she would never be ready for anything again.

Morgan opened a book and read. Mrs. Santa clicked away at her knitting. Finally the public address system crackled, "Attention all passengers headed eastbound to Reno, Salt Lake City, Denver, Chicago, and points in between. The *California Zephyr* is pulling into the station and will be ready for boarding momentarily."

The teenager snapped her phone shut with a pout and joined her parents. Her father was bald, and her mother was wearing a straw sombrero with "Chevy's" stitched on the front in red.

When Morgan stood up, the redheaded twins broadsided her and knocked her back into her seat. Their mother screamed from the door, "Get over here right now or I'm leaving you."

Morgan buttoned her raincoat and towed her suitcases after the crowd. The teenager's father, who had dropped back to smoke a last cigarette, watched her struggle to get her bags up the steps to the train. He took pity on her, ground out his cigarette, carried her bags up the steps, and stashed them for her.

She made her way down the narrow aisle between seats in the coach car. It was a tight squeeze. The only seats that were open were the two directly across from the twins and their mother. The twins were kneeling in the window seat, bouncing up and down and pulverizing graham crackers against the glass.

Morgan slid into the window seat opposite them and put her purse and shoulder bag on the seat next to her. The mother of the twins leaned across and said, "Just so you know, that aisle seat is ours."

Morgan nodded, moved her things to her lap, and stared down at her puffy ankles. She raised her footrest and tried to reach down to rub them, but her big belly blocked the way. She turned her face to the window and waited.

An observer might have thought that Morgan was listing

the many ways her child would be different from the little terrors across the aisle, but this was not the case. Her concern extended no lower than her own bruised heart. It was as if the baby inside her, almost full term, was just catching a ride with her, just hitchhiking to Denver in the same body she happened to inhabit.

When the train shrieked and lurched into motion, the twins went wild. Morgan pressed foam plugs into her ears, and watched the backs of houses, rusted swing sets, fenced-in Dobermans, and stacks of old furniture pass by her window.

People in their backyards stopped what they were doing when the train passed. A woman kneeling in her garden set down her trowel, a boy stopped pedaling his tricycle, two men working on a boat lifted their heads. All of them turned toward the train and waved, and Morgan waved back. She began to feel like they were waving to her personally and wishing her a good trip. She half expected them to yell, "Call me when you get there," and that made her cry because of course they didn't care what kind of trip she was having or when she was going to get there, and neither did anyone else.

When the train left the suburbs and moved into open countryside, the steady green outside her window and the gentle rocking of the train lulled Morgan to sleep. The next thing she knew, the dining car steward was shouting, "First call for lunch in the dining car. That's through this door and three cars back. First call for lunch!"

She could smell bananas and grease as the twins and their mother broke out their lunch, and she longed to get away from them, but she was too groggy to drag herself to the dining car. She ate dried apricots and raw cashews from a plastic bag in her purse and then fell back into an uncomfortable sleep and dreamed she had to run with a raw egg balanced on a spoon in a race where there was a great deal at stake.

She dozed and read for the rest of the afternoon, depending on the din from across the aisle. When she woke up at five, the twins and their mother were gone. She felt a rush of hope, but then she saw two plastic pistols in the pile of potato chip bags and banana peels on the floor, and she knew they'd be back.

The train was high in the Sierras by then, and snowflakes were blowing against the window. Gradually the dark green pines turned black, and by six, moonlight was sparkling on deep snow.

The twins came screaming down the aisle and collided with the dining car steward, who yelped, "First call for dinner." This time Morgan didn't hesitate. She struggled to her feet and lurched down the aisle before the twins could lift their pistols.

In the dining car, the steward seated her next to the rosy-cheeked woman who had watched her bags in the station back in Emeryville, and for a few moments Morgan felt that things were looking up.

She scanned the menu greedily. She was hungry enough to eat three dinners, but she knew she'd have to settle for one. There wasn't much room in her stomach because of the hitch-hiker who was pressing up from below.

"Tired, dear?" the woman beside her asked.

"Yes," Morgan said and waited for the woman to give the details of the final months of her own pregnancies.

"I'm going to have the pork tenderloin," the woman said. "I shouldn't, but we are on vacation, aren't we?" She winked at Morgan.

"I think I'll have that too," Morgan said.

The parents of the teenager entered the dining car, and the steward seated them at Morgan's table. The father nodded at the two women and said, "Skip Mills."

Morgan thought he said, "Skip meals," and she was unsure how to respond. Was he saying she'd gained too much weight with the pregnancy?

She frowned at him, but he continued, "And this is my wife, Nancy. We're headed home to Omaha."

"I'm Esther Robinson," said the rosy-cheeked woman.

"Morgan," Morgan said.

"So when are you due?" Nancy asked Morgan.

"In January," Morgan said.

"I'm surprised your doctor let you travel, this far along," Nancy said.

"Oh, you know how they are these days. Work up until the day you deliver; go home from the hospital the next day," Morgan said. Actually, her obstetrician had refused to give her a note to fly to Colorado, and that's why she was on the train, but she considered this none of Nancy's business.

"What are you knitting?" Morgan asked Esther to prevent Nancy from presenting unappetizing details of her own pregnancies and deliveries.

Esther laughed. "It's a Christmas sweater for our hound dog."

Morgan wanted to put her head on Esther's shoulder and take a nap while they waited for dinner. She wanted Skip and Nancy to disappear until the train arrived in Denver; then Skip could materialize long enough to help her get her suitcases off the train.

A waiter came and took their orders. As soon as he left, Nancy asked, "So where's your husband?"

There was a long silence. Morgan blushed and stared down at the navy blue Amtrak logo on her paper place mat. "I'd rather not talk about it," she said softly.

"The bastard!" Nancy said.

Morgan bit her lip and looked out the window. Warmed by

Nancy's sympathy, she was fighting back an impulse to tell her and Skip and Esther the whole story, but she stopped herself. People from Des Moines and Omaha might not be ready to hear that it was a bitch rather than a bastard who did this to her.

Instead she asked Esther, "What kind of dog do you have?"

"A basset hound," Esther said."

"We've got a German shepherd," Skip volunteered. "More of a watchdog than a pet. Maybe you ought to knit Butch a sweater, Nance."

"Sure," Nancy said, "and you put it on him."

"He's not really a people dog," Skip explained. "Too bad, too. I got him as a pet for our daughter, Tiffany."

"You did not. You got him to guard your goddamn boat," Nancy said.

"Excuse me," Morgan said, and she left the table, hurried down the aisle, and exited the dining car. She was back in kindergarten, running toward the bathroom, too late, too late.

In a tiny bathroom on the lower level of her coach car, she sat down on the toilet. Her maternity jeans and her stretched-out underpants were soaked, but not with urine. An odor she'd never smelled before filled the air. It smelled like metal rusting in marsh water.

Her heart pounded in her ears. This was it. Her bag of waters had broken, so the baby was going to come soon. But it doesn't happen right away, she told herself, not like in the movies. There's still time. I can make it to Denver. First babies take a long time.

She checked her watch and then pulled a timetable out of her purse. It was 6:30, and the waiter who'd taken their order said they'd be in Reno shortly. The train was running two hours late, so she'd be in Denver by 9:30 the next morning. It would be soon enough. She didn't feel even a twinge of cramping. She was sure she could make it, in light of the alternatives. She wasn't about to get off and have a baby in a hospital room with slot machines in the corner. Besides, she didn't have insurance, so they probably wouldn't let her through the door. She had to make it to Denver, where her sister knew a midwife who could help her have the baby at home.

Morgan waited till the coast was clear and waddled to the baggage shelves, where she pulled some clean underwear and a fresh pair of maternity jeans out of her suitcase. She stepped into the tiny shower compartment and changed her clothes. She paused, wondering what to do with the soaked pants that she'd removed. They were too smelly to leave in the wastebasket, so although she hated to litter, she flung them off the platform between cars.

The freezing wind snatched them into the darkness. Morgan's white underpants soared off on their own, like an owl on night business, and her maternity jeans flapped through the snow until they were impaled on a fence. The waist caught on the barbs of the upper wire, and the legs snagged on the barbs of the lower. Future passengers on the Zephyr would see Morgan's dark blue pants stretched taut against the empty sky and wonder who had hung them there and why.

"Good. You're back," Esther said to Morgan when she got back to the table. "Don't let your dinner get cold."

Morgan ate with gusto. She hoped nobody smelled anything.

"So what's it like?" Nancy asked Esther.

Esther turned to Morgan. "I was just telling them about my roomette. I feel like the Queen of Sheba! My back was so bad this fall that the folks back home took up a collection and got me a private sleeper."

"We should have got one of those," Nancy said, giving Skip a scornful sideways look. He ignored her and kept chewing a large bite of well-done steak.

"Of course, it's just the standard, not the deluxe, but it's real cozy," Esther said. "I praise the Lord that I've got it. I'm worn out from the big showdown we had at the Corps."

"Are you in the military?" Morgan asked.

Esther smiled. "Yes, I am. I'm a Senior Soldier in the Salvation Army."

Morgan felt a touch of vertigo. The train was taking her back where she had come from, and though she'd been gone for only three years, it felt like she was entering foreign and dangerous territory.

"It's the Army that sent me to San Francisco," Esther said. "To protest. The city government there told our San Francisco Corps they couldn't get any city money unless they gave health benefits to domestic partners."

"To who?" Skip asked.

"The gays," Nancy told him.

"Well," Esther continued, "the head officer was about to give in. All of the other organizations in San Francisco were going along with it, even churches. But that's when we put our foot down. Grass roots, all over the country, soldiers in the Salvation Army said no."

Morgan felt queasy. Her hands and feet felt cold.

Esther sat straighter and taller, warming to her subject. "Enough is enough," she said. "We had to lay down the law."

"Our waiter at Chevy's was gay," Nancy said. "He was sweet to me when I spilled my margarita, and he gave me a sombrero for free even though it wasn't my birthday."

"We don't have anything against the gays," Esther said. "It's the principle of the thing. We don't give health benefits to any partners except married partners. Gay or not gay."

"The difference is," Morgan said in a squeaky voice, "the not gays can get married." She reached for her water glass, but her hands were shaking, and she knocked it over.

"There, there, dear," Esther said and handed over her napkin for the spill. "God will look after the gays, just like he's going to look after you. He hates the sin but loves the sinner." She patted Morgan's shoulder. "The Lord works in mysterious ways, and he's standing right behind you. I can feel him there."

"Reno!" the conductor announced, and the train stopped in the middle of downtown. Morgan felt a mild contraction. It occurred to her that maybe she should get off after all, take whatever Reno had to offer in the way of hospitals, and put it on her credit card. Then she looked at the faces of the people on the sidewalks, their skin tinted garish colors by the neon as they scuttled from casino to casino on Christmas Eve, and she decided to stay on the train. At least she'd shared a meal with these strangers, and if she really started having contractions, she could get off in Winnemucca in a few hours.

As the train pulled out of Reno, the waiter brought dessert, and Morgan lost herself in a wedge of hot apple pie a la mode. She took tiny bites, trying to make it last a long time so she wouldn't have to go back to her seat, but other passengers were lined up, waiting impatiently for tables.

"Let's retire to the observation car," Esther said, and they all stood up and followed her there. They sat in a row on swivel chairs, watching Reno thin out and fade away. Johnny Mathis sang a barely audible *White Christmas* over the PA system.

After they passed through Sparks, Nevada, Morgan went downstairs to pee. The ladies' bathroom had a lounge area with a well-lit mirror over a stainless steel vanity counter. When Morgan came out of the bathroom, she found Nancy sitting at the vanity pouring a can of mai tai mix into a plastic cup with ice in it.

"I'm afraid to drink in front of Esther," she said

"I'm afraid to exist in front of Esther," Morgan said. She sat down at the vanity and winced at her blotchy skin and the dark circles under her eyes. She ran her palm across her half-inch-long hair and turned away from the mirror.

"Excuse me for asking this, but are you gay?" Nancy said.

"Yes," Morgan said.

"I thought so. Your hair, and that conversation at dinner."

"Since I've gotten pregnant, nobody thinks I'm a lesbian. It's awful. Before, I was a big butch."

"That's our dog's name," Nancy said.

"I know," Morgan said.

"I hate that dog," Nancy said.

"People used to be afraid of me," Morgan said. "Now they come up and rub my belly."

"Yeah, it changes you. Skip says I turned into my mother the second I got pregnant."

"Shot full of estrogen," Morgan said. "It's made me soft. I let strangers rub my belly."

Nancy finished her mai tai and took another canned mai tai out of her bag and poured it into her glass. "Too bad you can't drink," she said.

"You can say that again. Can I smell it?"

"Sure," Nancy said and handed it over.

The scent of rum in Nancy's drink took Morgan back to college football games, rum and Coke in a thermos, frozen fingers on the red plastic thermos lid, the burn of the rum as it went down. And later, in bars, other rum drinks, all kinds of drinks in women's bars, drinking a lot to get up the nerve to ask for phone numbers, borrowing pens from bartenders and writing numbers on matchbook covers in the dark. And later still, drinking hot buttered rum in front of a huge fireplace after skiing with Judith, feeling the sweet heat of it all the way to her toes and fingertips, reaching over to interlace her fingers with Judith's.

Morgan handed the mai tai back to Nancy. The smell of rum and the rocking of the train had created a certain coziness, and Morgan began to feel close to Nancy, secure in the intimacy that can spring up between travelers anywhere, but most especially on a train in the middle of nowhere at night.

"On Halloween," Morgan told Nancy, "I didn't go to the Castro with Judith because it's too crazy there when you're sober. Judith went with our friend Marcie instead. They're both phlebotomists, so they wore their hospital scrubs and vampire teeth and went around tying surgical tubing around people's necks and pretending to suck their blood. They were a big hit. At least that's what Judith told me when she came roaring in at three a.m. I got mad at her for waking me up, but she didn't apologize. She said, 'I'm sick of reading baby books and refinishing antique baby furniture. I want to have a little fun.'

"'What about our baby?' I asked, and she said, 'Whose baby?'"

"Well," Nancy said, "whose baby is it?"

"I thought it was mine and Judith's. We got the sperm from Eddie, a gay guy at the bookstore where I worked, but he was never going to be the father. Just the donor."

"Skip always wanted to be a father. I wasn't so sure I wanted to have kids. Maybe like your girlfriend. I had two miscarriages before we had Tiffany, and it nearly killed him. He's spoiled her for her whole life, it was so hard to get her."

Morgan put her hands on her stomach. "I talked to this baby all day long from Easter until Thanksgiving. Maybe too much. I know Judith felt left out sometimes.

"She had to work on Thanksgiving, so I went to Eddie's house for dinner. He was doing a huge production for eight guys and me, and he got hysterical when he found out he didn't have any nutmeg for the pumpkin pies. I went over to our place to get some. While I was in the kitchen, I heard giggling coming from the bedroom. I tiptoed down the hall, and there was Judith lying on top of Marcie in our bed."

"Shit," Nancy said. "What did you do?"

"I screamed, 'You call this *working?*' Marcie flew out of bed and cowered in the corner, and Judith got up on her knees and clasped her hands and whimpered, 'I'm sorry, I'm sorry, I'm sorry, I'm sorry.' If I hadn't been in shock and chock-full of hormones, I probably would have hit her, but as it was, I burst into tears and ran out of the bedroom. At the front door, I remembered the nutmeg, and I went back and got it and took it to Eddie's.

"That night I felt like I was going to die. I didn't, but the baby and I sort of stopped speaking to each other.

"I shut myself into Eddie's back bedroom and cried for a week and a half. Then Judith called from Tahoe, where she'd gone skiing with Marcie, and she said she hoped we could all be friends. When she tried to give me Marcie's therapist's phone number, I ripped the telephone out of the wall and threw it across the room.

"Of course I paid to fix the phone, but then I cried for another couple of weeks, and finally Eddie couldn't take it anymore, so I called my sister in Denver. She said I could go there, even though her husband can't stand me, but by then they wouldn't let me fly, so here I am."

An industrial-strength contraction seized Morgan, and she let out a moan. "I feel like I need to lie down," she told Nancy.

Nancy helped her up the stairs to the observation car, where Skip and Esther were sitting side by side watching snow whirl in the yard lights of lonely ranch houses along the track.

"Quite a storm," Esther said. "I'm glad I'm not out there driving in it."

"Morgan needs to lie down," Nancy said to Esther.

"I'll bet she does, poor dear. Now that you mention it, I do too," Esther said and stood up. "Well, goodnight all. Maybe we'll meet at breakfast." She gave them a brisk smile and left.

"I was hoping she'd offer that roomette she was bragging about," Nancy said.

"Thanks," Morgan said. "Winnemucca's only a couple of hours away. I'll get off there."

"I thought you were going to Denver," Skip said.

"She's having contractions," Nancy said.

"Holy Toledo," Skip said and jumped up. "Here, let us help you back to your seat. The coach seats aren't too bad when you recline them all the way. Do you have a blanket and pillow?"

Morgan shook her head.

"We'll get them for you," Skip said and led the way toward the coach cars.

Morgan sat down with Nancy while Skip looked for an attendant. Across the aisle, Tiffany was asleep with her headphones on, and Nancy reached across and took them out of her ears and turned off her CD player. She brushed a strand of hair out of Tiffany's face and tucked it behind her ear. Then she pulled the blanket on her lap up around her shoulders. The tenderness stirred something in Morgan and made her feel she could make it to Winnemucca.

Skip finally returned with two blankets and three pillows. Before Morgan could get to her feet, metal screeched against metal, and a series of jolts passed through the train. Skip lost his footing and sprawled out in the aisle. Other passengers cried out as they were catapulted against the seats in front of them. Skip crawled over to check that Tiffany and Nancy and Morgan were all right, and then he went up the aisle to see if anyone needed help.

"He was a medic in the Navy," Nancy said. "He feels like he

owes the whole world first aid."

"That's great," Morgan said.

Nancy raised her eyebrows. "It is? I always thought it was a sort of hero-to-the rescue, pain-in-the-butt thing."

"No," Morgan said. "It's a beautiful thing."

Nancy looked up the aisle at her husband, who was putting his rolled-up sweatshirt behind the neck of an old man who had a nosebleed. She smiled at him, a smile that lit up her face, and he waved and grinned back at her.

Morgan doubled over in pain. Finally she couldn't keep from letting out a loud groan.

"Are you all right?" Nancy asked. "Did you hit your stomach?"

"I don't think I hit my stomach," Morgan said, "but I'm having whopping big contractions now."

Nancy said, "Tiffany, go get your father."

When Tiffany and Skip came back, Nancy told Skip, "That old biddy in the roomette has to let Morgan lie down. Let's go."

Nancy got up and helped Skip pull Morgan to her feet.

"Bring your purse and your CD player," she told Tiffany, and the four of them fought their way back through the aisles of three coaches, through the dining car, and through the observation car. Rumors were flying all around them. Derailment. Hit a truck. Drunk engineer pulled the wrong handle.

An attendant stopped them inside the door of the sleeping car.

"We're here to see Esther Robinson," Nancy told him.

"She didn't say anything about visitors to me," he said, but he led them to the end of the car and stopped in front of a sliding glass door with a curtain drawn across it.

Nancy tapped on the glass and called out, "Esther! Are you all right?"

Esther pulled back the curtain. She was wearing a flannel nightgown, and she had a brown net over her hair. When she saw who they were, she slid the door open. "My, that was some bump," she said. "What happened?"

"Snowdrift derailed the freight train in front of us," the attendant said. "We're not going anywhere tonight. They'll have to dig us out in the morning."

"Where are we?" Morgan asked him.

"I'd say we're just about exactly halfway between a rock and a hard place," he said and laughed at his own joke. "No, actually, we're about halfway between Sparks and Winnemucca. They'll probably send a crew out from Sparks."

"Well, I'm about to have a baby, and it feels like it's going to happen before they can dig us out."

"Holy shit. We can't get an ambulance or even a helicopter out here in a storm like this. Who let you on the train in this condition? Where did you get on anyway?"

"I don't think that really matters now, does it?" Skip said. "Why don't you just bring us a first aid kit?"

Esther sat on her bed with pursed lips and folded arms.

"Esther," Nancy said, "the people up there in the coach cars are really shaken up. They could use your help. Otherwise they're going to be heading for the bar car, and we all know what that could turn into."

Esther closed the curtain of her compartment. Tiffany listened to her CD player and popped her gum in time to a song that nobody else could hear. Morgan leaned against the wall and grimaced with each new wave of pain. Nancy slipped her arm around Skip's waist, and he put his arm around her shoulders and pulled her in close. They all watched the glass door of the compartment, waiting for a sign, and they were not disappointed. The curtain twitched, and rustling and thumping came from within.

Moments later, Esther threw back the curtain and emerged through the sliding glass door in full uniform. She had on a navy blue skirted suit with red epaulets on the shoulders of the jacket and a red S on each lapel. She was wearing navy pumps and a perky blue cap.

"Cool," Tiffany said, and the adults nodded in agreement.

"Use my room," Esther told Morgan. "I won't be needing it." She marched toward the front of the train, and the others cheered.

Thus it was that Esther took on the most difficult mission of her life. She calmed three coaches full of weary travelers who were gradually realizing they were going to spend Christmas on a train without heat. She led them in singing *Hark! The Herald, Angels Sing*, and *Joy To The World.* She organized the kitchen crew to hand out free, healthy snacks. Most important, she single-handedly prevented a vigilante group from flinging a single mother and her redheaded twins off the train.

And thus it was that in Room 6 on the stalled *Zephyr* on Christmas Eve, Nancy and Skip labored with Morgan and drew closer to each other than they had been for sixteen years, and Tiffany saw with her own eyes where babies come from and swore she would never have one.

And thus it was that Morgan spoke to her baby after a month of silence, and she said, "You can come out now—we're safe," and then, "Come out now," and then "Come out! Now!"

And thus it was that many hours later, just as the sun rose over the icy desert, the baby forgave his mother for deserting him and slid out into this world somewhere between a rock and a hard place.